Augustin Daly, Albin Valafrègue

Love in Harness

A Comedy in Three Acts

Augustin Daly, Albin Valafrègue

Love in Harness
A Comedy in Three Acts

ISBN/EAN: 9783744784436

Printed in Europe, USA, Canada, Australia, Japan

Cover: Foto ©Andreas Hilbeck / pixelio.de

More available books at **www.hansebooks.com**

LOVE

IN

HARNESS

A COMEDY IN THREE ACTS

(From the French of Albin Valabregue)

AUGUSTIN DALY

ORIGINALLY PRODUCED AT DALY'S THEATRE, NOVEMBER 16, 1886

PRIVATELY PRINTED (AS MANUSCRIPT ONLY)

FOR THE AUTHOR

CAST OF THE ORIGINAL PRODUCTION, NOVEMBER 16, 1886.

MR. JEREMIAH JOBLOTS, who has happily married off two daughters and is despatching a third.....MR. CHARLES FISHER

MR. JULIUS NAGGITT, with a diary of matrimonial grievances ....MR. JAMES LEWIS

MR. FREDERICK URQUHART, with a single connubial complaint...Mr. JOHN DREW

CHARLEY HOFFMAN, M.D., who is undeterred by every warning ....MR. OTIS SKINNER

JOHN SCHLAGG, Urquhart's valet ....MR. WILLIAM GILBERT

KEYES, a piano-tuner................. ....MR. FREDERICK BOND

MRS. JULIANA JOBLOTS, a model mamma, with implicit confidence in her "Matrimonial Manual"..MRS. G. H. GILBERT

UNA URQUHART, a victim of jealousy and slave to the Manual ....MISS ADA REHAN

RHODA NAGGITT, a victim of her own making,
MISS VIRGINIA DREHER

JENNY JOBLOTS, a philosopher of nineteen....MISS LILLIAN HADLEY

MYRTILLA, incidental domestic on the scene of a domestic incident.......................MISS LIZZIE ST. QUENTIN

ANTOINETTE, Una's French maid and partner in a new Franco-German alliance........................MISS JEAN GORDON

SARAH, servant at Joblots'.....................MISS GRACE FILKINS

BEAUCIE ....BY THE ORIGINAL

ACT I.

MORNING ROOM AT JOBLOTS'.—The Harness Snaps and the Traces are Kicked Over.

ACT II.

PARLORS AT URQUHART'S.—A Double Runaway and Complete Smash-up.

ACT III.

NAGGITT'S BACHELOR FLAT.—The Old Harness is Mended and Another Set Ordered.

SCENE—NEW YORK.   TIME—LAST SPRING.

*** After the First Act the lapse of a fortnight is to be supposed.

ACT I.

Scene.—*Sitting- and music-room at Joblots' residence on the avenue. Piano in an alcove at back, R. Fireplace at L., with window above it on L. Main entrance, L. C. Door at R. up stage and another down stage. Table down, L.*

Keyes, *the piano-tuner, is discovered at the piano. His hat and umbrella are on a chair, c., near by.* Sarah *is dusting and replacing ornaments on the cabinet at c.*

Keyes. [*Tapping the keys to see if all are right.*] All right. There! You may hammer away again! This last daughter has a heavy hand at her music.

Sarah. [L.] She won't thump much longer in this house, she won't.

Keyes. [*Coming forward after shutting the piano.*] No? Why?

Sarah. [*Coming forward.*] Going to be married in six weeks.

Keyes. Miss Jenny going to be married, eh? [*Taking up his hat and umbrella from chair,* c.] What luck they have with their girls in this house—eh? Two gone and the last going. [*Exits,* L.]

Sarah. Did you know the others?

Keyes. Know 'em! Why, I've tuned that piano for fifteen years. It has suffered that length of time to my certain knowledge. [*Drops in chair,* c.] I was always called in to put the instrument in order when the beaux began their visits. First there was Miss Rhoda—she's Mrs. Naggitt now. Never plays any more. I tune her up for a party now and then, but anyone can see she's glad to be rid of it.

Sarah. They are all the same.

Keyes. Then there was Miss Una. [*Rises, gets,* R.] What a pair of thorough-goers she and her husband are. No going-to-sleep-o'-nights in that house. It's a regular vortex, it is.

Sarah. [*Going up a little.*] That's what I like.

Keyes. Do you? And now I'm a-tuning the venerable once more for Miss Jenny. When did you say she was going off— in six weeks?

Sarah. Six weeks—at least as far as I could overhe— [*Checks herself.*] ascertain.

Keyes. Exactly.

Sarah. Sh! Here she is. [*Busies herself at bric-à-brac, and* KEYES *steps up stage as* JENNY *enters from* R. *door. She is quite a young girl, dressed in white, blue ribbon sash, etc.*]

Jenny. Is everything all right now, Mr. Keyes?

Keyes. [*Crosses to her.*] I think you'll find it in good order, miss. [*She opens the piano and runs over the scale.* KEYES *listens approvingly with his hand to his ear.*]

Jenny. [*Plays a scale.*] Thank you. It's very nice. [SARAH *taps* KEYES *on the shoulder and points to arch,* L. C.]

Keyes. You are improving wonderfully. Wonderfully!

Jenny. Thank you. Good-morning!

Keyes. Good-morning! [*He steps out,* L. C., *embarrassed, after a nod to* SARAH.]

Jenny. Sarah! [*Runs over the scales.*] Sarah! Where's papa?

Sarah. In the library, writing. He's been writing all the morning.

Jenny. Then I'll play for him. He loves to have me play for him.

Sarah. Yes, miss. And he's going to lose you so soon.

Jenny. Go along, Sarah. [*Begins to play.*]

Sarah. Yes, miss. [*Begins to dance off to the polka which* JENNY *plays, but* JENNY *breaks down and* SARAH *stops.* JENNY *begins again, and* SARAH *recommences her dance, but as* JENNY *breaks down again in the same place* SARAH *stops and trudges off in disgust at* R. U. *door.* JENNY *tries once more and again breaks down in the same place. She half turns on the piano-stool and faces front.*]

Jenny. It does seem as if I never could get music into my head or out of my fingers. Only papa loves so much to hear me play, I wouldn't practise a bit more. [*She recommences the polka with the same break-down, and at this collapse* MR. JOBLOTS *enters* R. *with his hands to his ears, papers in his grasp, and a pen in his mouth and spectacles on his head. He takes one or two turns up and down, with a look of distress, as* JENNY *begins once more, her head close down to the music.*]

Joblots. [*Crosses to,* L., *table.*] I'm sorry; I declare I'm sorry that I ever allowed her to take lessons. [*Sits at table,* L., *and puts his papers on it and tries to foot up a column of figures, but in vain. Then, aloud to* JENNY.] My darling! Do try something else.

Jenny. Oh! is that you, papa? Did you hear me playing for you?

Job. Ye—es. [*She is going to begin again.*] Jenny, darling! Never mind playing any more! Come and give me a kiss.

Jenny. Wait one moment. [*Closes piano.*]

Job. I don't want to fatigue you. [*She runs and sits on his knee and kisses him.*] What do you think I'm busy at now?

Jenny. My wedding! [*Claps her hands.*]

Job. Yes, I've got to talk to young Hoffman's father to-day, and I'm drawing up an inventory of my little piggy-wiggy's little fortune. Just listen. [*As he is about to read,* MRS. JOB-LOTS *enters,* R.] Fifty shares B. & O., eighty Brooklyn water bonds, seventy-five——

Mrs. Joblots. [R.] Well, Jenny, your piano! [*Jenny turns, half towards her mother.*]

Job. Oh, Lord! I thought I'd got it over for the day!

Jenny. I'm talking to papa. [*Embraces him.*]

Job. I was giving her some needed explanations, and was about to impress on her that the Married Woman's Act gives a wife control of everything.

Jenny. [C.] Of her husband, too?

Job. Well, to the extent of preventing him from squandering her money!

Jenny. [*A step towards* MRS. JOBLOTS.] If there's any fear of that, why do you let me marry?

Mrs. J. We have the fullest confidence in young Dr. Hoffman. Your father is simply taking precautions.

Job. Your future husband belongs to an excellent family, and is worth a tidy little sum, and with your dowry——

Jenny. Besides what he makes at his profession——

Job. Doctor! Yes! His fees last year amounted to three hundred dollars. If the whooping-cough breaks out in your neighborhood you'll be millionnaires.

Mrs. J. [*Crosses,* C.] You're always joking, Jeremiah, dear.

Job. [*Rises.*] Yes, dear.

Jenny. [R.] Charley has a number of wealthy patients, papa.

Job. Yes, only they are never sick. They are honorary patients. Those that are sick are not wealthy. They are deadheads.

Jenny. But Charley told me——

Mrs. J. Don't "Charley" him so much, darling. Say

" Doctor Hoffman," or occasionally "Charles." It sounds better before people. [*Crosses*, R., *sits*. JOBLOTS *sits*, L.]

Jenny. Very well, mamma! [*To* JOBLOTS.] Well, papa, Doctor Charley—Charles, I mean—told me that he intends to become a specialist. He can charge double then.

Job. [L.] But he'll get only half the work. No, no; he'd better take his victims where he finds them. Let him cure everything. Don't be modest.

Jenny. Oh, you're always joking, papa.

Mrs. J. Yes. We'll see how you'll laugh six weeks from now—when she's married.

Jenny. [*Running to her.*] The fifteenth of May.

Job. [*Gravely, with a sigh.*] I wish it were six years off—or sixty.

Jenny. [*Pats his cheek.*] I'll run in and see you every day.

Job. [*Gazing in reverie before him.*] When I come home in the evening you won't be there. Who'll hand me my slippers, and cut all my books?

Mrs. J. [*Sighing, same.*] And what will I do without my lazy little girl to wake up with a kiss every morning?

Job. Who'll sugar my coffee and pour out my tea? [JENNY *runs over to him.*]

Mrs. Job. Who'll play the piano for us after dinner?

Job. [*Changing.*] Hm! Well, that's not so much consequence.

Mrs. J. [*Rises.*] Jeremiah, love, you're a heathen.

Job. Yes, dear. [*Rises—to* JENNY.] Don't forget to take your piano with you. We will not have any further use for it —when you go. Your mother—thank goodness—doesn't play. [*Crosses*, c.] You and your mother will never know what I have suffered from that instrument.

Jenny. [L.] Oh, papa!

Mrs. J. Jeremiah!

Job. I have had three daughters—and the scales—the four-hand pieces—the variations—[*Sees them grave.*] Are you angry? [*Takes each round the waist.*] I take it all back—but run off and fix yourself a little. Doctor Hoffman will be here presently. [*Crosses*, L. JENNY *goes*, R.]

Mrs. J. [*Stopping her.*] It will be your first interview, dear.

Jenny. [R.] Why, I've seen him lots of times, ma.

Mrs. J. It will be the first time you receive him alone—and out of our sight, darling.

Jenny. [R.] It will seem so funny. He and you always did the talking. What *shall* I say to him?

Job. [L.] Hem! Well, talk on indifferent topics.

Mrs. J. Be simple and natural. Be yourself, and whenever you find yourself in doubt as to what to say or do, consult this little book. [*Takes a small volume out of her pocket.*] I told you I would look it up for you. I gave a copy to each of your sisters before they were married, and they followed it implicitly, they always assured me.

Job. Oho! Oh, yes! "The Matrimonial Manual, or Hints to Hymen." [*Up.*]

Mrs. J. [C.] It provides for every emergency.

Jenny. Oh! do let me see it.

Mrs. J. [*Crossing, lays book on table,* L.] No; run and get ready. You'll find it here on the table.

Jenny. Oh, what fun! [*Exits skipping,* R. 1 E.]

Job. The idea! What's the use of that book? You and I were married without a "Matrimonial Manual," and everything went all right.

Mrs. J. Times are different. You can't be too cautious nowadays. It is a most valuable guide to young girls in those trying situations which precede marriage. It was very useful to Rhoda and Una.

Job. [*Crosses,* R.] That reminds me—I must send for Rhoda and give her a scolding.

Mrs. J. For what?

Job. She doesn't give her poor husband a moment's peace.

Mrs. J. It's his fault. He humors her too much.

Job. That's a good fault. And yet she gives him no rest. She's a perfect despot; not only compels him to obey her whims, but studies hard to thwart him in every particular.

Mrs. J. What a contrast to poor Una and her tyrant. He prevents her receiving her friends, and won't let her go into society. That girl is perfectly wretched. *I* shall have a talk with *him.* [*Crosses,* R.]

Job. Don't you meddle with it. You'll accomplish nothing, and your interference will be set down as another case of mother-in-law. [*Shakes his head.*] Ah, the trouble with both households is the want of a nursery. A home without children is a room without fire. You congeal! it's perpetual winter! Wait till we lose our Jenny, and you'll feel as if the blaze on our own hearth had gone out. I want grandchildren to warm me up in my old age. When we see the chubbies playing on our carpet, we'll forget our gray hairs. We'll always have one of them home with us—the one that bawls the loudest—to remind us of the first years of our own marriage—eh? What say you, old helpmate? Shan't we?

Mrs. J. Yes, dear. Well, let's hope for the best. But in these family quarrels it does seem to me as though Una and Rhoda haven't good sense. Why dispute continually with one's husband? Why?

Job. Especially with such good husbands.

Mrs. J. And such chums! Almost like brothers.

Job. Yes, dear! and so prosperous! [SARAH *enters*, L. C.]

Sarah. Please'm—Mr.—Mr.—[*Forgets name.*] Mr.—[*With a burst.*] Miss Jenny's young gentleman. [JOBLOTS *takes stage.*]

Mrs. J. [R.] [*Severely.*] Have you forgotten the doctor's name, Sarah?

Sarah. Please'm—Doctor Charley——

Mrs. J. What?

Sarah. · I heard Miss Jenny call him——

Mrs. J. Show Dr. Hoffman in.

Sarah. Yes'm. [*Going, beating her breast to remember.*] Dr. Hoffman, Dr. Hoffman, Dr. Hoffman. [*Exit*, L. C.]

Mrs. J. [*Turning toward door*, R.] That new girl is the hardest to break in we've had this winter. [JENNY *enters*, R. 1 E.]

Jenny. Here I am, ma.

Mrs. J. I was just about to send for you.

Jenny. I saw him coming from the window.

Job. [*To* MRS. JOBLOTS.] Come, my dear.

Mrs. J. [*Going up.*] We'll leave you together. [JENNY *gets*, L.]

Job. Be natural.

Mrs. J. Be yourself! [*They exeunt*, R. *arch.*]

Jenny. What shall I do? What shall I say? Oh, dear!

Sarah. [*Enters*, L. C., *announcing.*] Dr. Hoffman!

Hoffman. [*Enters*, C.; *puts hat on chair*, L. C.] Good-morning, Miss Jenny. [*About to sit, recollects his hat, and puts it on table*, L. JENNY, *much embarrassed, bows, stammers, puts her hand to her throat.* SARAH *exits.*] Are your mother and father quite well?

Jenny. [R.] Quite—quite, thank you. [*Aside.*] He looks as if he didn't mind it a bit.

Hoff. Jenny! Dear Jenny! Do you know, this is the very first time I have had you all alone by myself. Isn't it like beginning house-keeping? Let's commence our apprenticeship.

Jenny. [*Nervous.*] Oh, yes—but—[*Aside.*] I haven't had time to look at the Manual. [*Crosses*, L., *edges to table, sits, and gets book, which she opens furtively, half turned away from* HOFFMAN.]

Hoff. [*Hurt.*] Why, Jenny—Jenny——

Jenny.   Yes!

Hoff.   [*Severely.*]   Do you love me?

Jenny.   [*Aside.*]   I don't know whether I ought to tell him yet. I wonder if that's in the book. [*Turns over the leaves aside.*]

Hoff.   [*Affectionately.*]   My darling, look at me!

Jenny.   Will you have the goodness to open the piano?

Hoff.   [*Aside, astonished.*]   She wants to play the Swedish wedding march for me again. [*Goes to piano.*]

Jenny.   [*Hastily turns over leaves and reads.*]   "First *tête-à-tête* the day after marriage." [*Speaks.*] That isn't it! [*Turns back leaves.*] Ah!

Hoff.   Shall I open the top?

Jenny.   Open everything! [*Aside, reads.*]   "First *tête-à-tête* after engagement." [*Speaks.*] That's it! [*Reads.*] "The young lady should be exceedingly reserved." [*Speaks.*] I was afraid so.

Hoff.   [R.]   [*Advancing.*]   Now, darling. The ivories are awaiting the alabaster.

Jenny.   All right. You can shut the piano!

Hoff.   [*Aside.*]   She does'nt know what she's about. Little darling! She's nervous. [*Goes back to piano.*]

Jenny.   [*Reading.*]   "And the young man should be affectionate"—[*Speaks.*] I knew that ought to be—[*Reads.*] "but not too demonstrative."

Hoff.   [*At piano.*]   Shall I shut the top?

Jenny.   [*Rises.*]   Shut everything.   [*Aside.*]   I ought to read the whole chapter.

Hoff.   [*After closing the piano.*] There! [*Advances. She drops on sofa. He sits beside her. She moves off, still consulting book. He advances nearer to her.*] You are not afraid of me?

Jenny.   No. [*Glances at book.*] You may be affectionate.

Hoff.   Of course. [*Shoves nearer to her.*]

Jenny.   But not too demonstrative.

Hoff.   Ah! [*Pause.*] Do you remember our first meeting? You were going to the Park with your mother. I was on my way to see a patient with typhus. You brought me luck. I saved him.

Jenny.   I congratulate you—and him.

Hoff.   [*Warmly.*] I loved you at first sight. [*Seizes her hand.*]

Jenny.   [*Drawing it away.*] Not too demonstrative. [*Rises; crosses,* L.]

Hoff.   But I must show my love. [*She crosses,* L., *and sits in a chair; he draws another chair and sits beside her, gradually get-*

ting nearer to her.]   Tell me about your girlhood—your sweet girlhood and your childhood—all about them.

Jenny.   What would you like to know about them ?

Hoff.   Were you ever sick ?   What did you have ?

Jenny.   [*Aside.*] His conversation is very technical.

Hoff.   I don't wish to lose a single detail of your early youth.   We will live the past over again together.   And the present it shall be my aim to make so delightful that it will charm us in turn when it too becomes the past.   [*Smiling.*]

Jenny.   [*Reading, aside.*]   "The most intelligent man will sometimes appear stupid at the first interview."

Hoff.   Why do you turn your head away ?

Jenny.   I was thinking.

Hoff.   [*Close to her.*] Let me see your lovely eyes ! Jenny, you are my ideal.   Before I knew you, when I had dreams of the being who would some day be my wife, it was your image I beheld, it was your heart which beat in her bosom.

Jenny.   [*Aside.*]   He's doing better.

Hoff.   How lovely you are to me !   [*Takes her hand.*]

Jenny.   [*Aside, rising.*]   He's getting on too fast.   [*Aloud.*] Not too demonstrative, Charles, please.

Hoff.   [*Retaining her hand in spite of a feeble struggle.*]   I can't help it, Jenny—I adore you.

Jenny.   [*Crosses,* R.]   But I'm sure you shouldn't go so far, so fast.   Listen.

Hoff.   Why ?

Jenny.   [*Reads from Manual.*]   "The young gentleman is likely to be somewhat reserved at the first interview alone, out of consideration for the delicacy of the young lady's feelings.   Yet a certain degree of emotion is permissible.   But his glances alone should express his ardor, until the marriage ceremony makes her his own.   See Note 1."   [*Speaks and explains to him.*]   Note 1: that means there's a note at the end of the book containing fuller details.   [*Turns to the last page and reads.*]   "Note 1.—For engagement and wedding presents, go to Johnston Brothers, Canal, corner Greene.   Presents from one dollar up."

Hoff.   That seems to be a very useful book.   [*Bends forward to look over the book, his hands clasped behind him ; rises, and points to the passage.*]

Jenny.   [*Reads from the cover.*]   It's called " Hints to Hymen ; or, the Woman's Matrimonial Manual—Every Couple their own Guide, Philosopher, and Friend."   [*Looks up.*]   It tells you everything.

Hoff.   Especially what shops to patronize.

Jenny. Let's look through it. [*Turns pages and reads.*]
"Part First—Engagement. [*He edges close to her.*] Part
Second—Marriage. [*He puts his arm around her waist.*] Part
Third—Widowhood. [*He drops his arm.*] Part Fourth—
Second Marriages." [*He turns away.*] Nice, isn't it? Pro-
vides for everything.

Hoff. Immense! Wish I had one. Does it say when a chap
can have a kiss?

Jenny. [*Without looking at the book.*] Once when he comes
to see her, and once when he is going.

Hoff. By Jove! I've been cheated. You must give me that
one for coming.

Jenny. Oh, no—I mustn't—you. [*He kisses her, and is about
to repeat it.*] Once! [*She puts her hand up between his face
and her own. He draws her hand down and kisses it.*]

Hoff. Couldn't you advance me a week's allowance?

Jenny. The idea! What would we have to-morrow?

Hoff. Don't let's borrow trouble. Providence will provide
for to-morrow. [*Kisses her.* MRS. JOBLOTS *enters,* R. *arch, and
surprises them.*]

Mrs. Joblots. Jenny! [HOFFMAN *puts* JENNY *to* L.] Once on
coming and once on going.

Hoff. This is the one on going. [*Puts chair up a little.*]
See, mamma, I am going now. [*Aside to* JENNY.] And in fifteen
minutes one for returning. [*Goes up to* MRS. JOBLOTS.] I hope
you are quite well. [*To* JOBLOTS, *who enters,* R. *arch.*] And you,
sir? [*Fumbles with his handkerchief quite nervously.*] Good-
morning, sir. Good-morning, Mrs. Joblots. Good-morning,
Miss Jenny. I'll be back presently. [*Exits,* L. C., *putting his
handkerchief on his head and trying to put his hat in his pocket.*]

Job. Well, daughter? Are you still glad that I gave my
consent?

Jenny. [L.] Yes, papa. But I've had enough of the Manual.
It's stuff. [*Crosses,* C.] I can get on just as well without it.

Job. What did the doctor have to say to you?

Jenny. He kissed me.

Mrs. J. [R.] Is that all you remember?

Sarah. [*Enters hurriedly,* L. C.] If you please, 'm, Miss Una's
here.

Mrs. J. [*Crosses to her.*] Miss—who?

Sarah. Beg pardon, 'm. Mrs. Urquhart. She's in the hall.

Job. [*Coolly.*] Well, why doesn't she come up?

Sarah. She told me to see if anybody was with you, because
she's been crying.

Mrs. J. My daughter crying!

Sarah. She's brought a lot of trunks and baggage, 'm.

Job. Trunks and baggage!

Mrs. J. [*Impatiently.*] Tell her to come up. [*Crosses to* JENNY. SARAH *exits*, L. C.]

Job. What can it mean? [UNA *enters*, L. C., *leading a little dog.* ANTOINETTE, *her French maid, follows with bird-cage and satchel.*]

Una. [*Suffocated with tears.*] Good-morning, mamma! [*Kisses her.*] Good-morning, papa! [*Kisses him.*] Good-morning, Jenny. Oh! oh! oh! [*Sits, and her tears redouble. All gather round her.* ANTOINETTE *stands at back of her chair.*]

Mrs. J. What has happened, child?

Sarah. [*Enters,* L. C.] What shall I do with the baggage?

Job. Don't bother us.

Una. [*Through her tears.*] Antoinette!

Antoinette. Oui, madame.

Una. Take care of Beaucie. He's all that's left me now except papa and mamma. [ANTOINETTE *hands cage to* SARAH, *who exits,* L. C., *with it, and picks up the dog and stands behind her mistress.*]

Job. Calm yourself, dear—calm yourself.

Una. [*Her voice choked with tears.*] Papa, I've come home again! For good!

Job. [*Turning to look at her.*] Come home again! For good!

Mrs. J. [R. C.] Another quarrel with your husband?

Una. [*Between sobs.*] It's nothing at all. Papa, you know what a sweet disposition I have, but life with that man is no longer possible. So I have left him forever.

Job. And you call that nothing at all?

Jenny. Why, Fred seemed to adore you.

Mrs. J. [*Turning to* JENNY.] You had better order some tea for your sister instead of standing there with your mouth and ears open. Don't you see how weak and agitated she is? [*Crosses,* R. *Sits on sofa.*]

Jenny. I'll get some right away. [*Going.*]

Job. [*Calling after her.*] Get three cups, Jenny. Your mother and I are equally agitated. [JENNY *exits,* R. U. E.] Now, then [*To* UNA], what is it all about?

Una. [*To* JOBLOTS, *through sobs.*] Papa, look at me; you see before you the most miserable creature in the whole world.

Job. You astonish me. But all you women say the same thing.

Una. [C.] Frederick doesn't understand me.

Job. [L.] Perhaps you express yourself badly.

Una. I knew how it would be. Love-matches always end this way.

Mrs. J. [R.] [*To* JOBLOTS.] They've had another quarrel. I was sure of it.

Una. A quarrel? That doesn't begin to express it. I don't know what to call it. We were invited last night to the Patriarch's Ball. I had ordered a most exquisite costume. Oh, such a gown! A robe of delicate blue velvet, with white lace. The waist *à la vierge* of trimmed velvet biassed, like this [*shows with her handkerchief*], with a garland of tea-roses. The skirt all lace on one side, the train of velvet, and looped up. [JOBLOTS *turns away, face to table, bewildered.*] In front a medallion of pearls, surrounded by Spanish point, dotted round like butterfly-wings. Can't you **see** the whole thing, mamma? It was just lovely. [JOBLOTS *turns to face her, throws himself back in his chair, his legs stretched, scratching his head.*]

Mrs. J. Perfectly, my dear! Perfectly.

Una. [*Perceiving* JOBLOTS *scratching his head and making a grimace.*] Now, look at papa. He acts as if he didn't understand a word I'm saying. [*Petulantly.*] It isn't worth while taking the trouble——

Job. [*Soothingly.*] Don't say that, daughter—don't say that.

Una. [*Sits*, C.] Well, Frederick came home, and, would you believe it?—he had forgotten all about the ball.

Ant. [*Advancing*, L. C.] It is ze naked, barefaced **truth.** Oui, madame is not exaggerate one bit at all.

Una. Antoinette! [ANTOINETTE *goes back.*] Hold your tongue! At ten o'clock, the time for dressing, he said to me: "Una, suppose we don't go to this ball?"

Job. I can understand that.

Una. I simply said: "You must be crazy! There's my dress." "Wear it somewhere next week," he said. "But it may be copied all over by that time." "Never mind. Give up this ball. Make a sacrifice for my sake," he said. You must know that every other word in my gentleman's mouth is sacrifice. Make some sacrifice for me! I refused. He insisted. I held my own.

Job. [*Calmly.*] And he gave in?

Una. [*To* JOBLOTS.] I should say so. But wait. We went to the ball. Then he commenced. After two o'clock, it was every other minute: "Una, shall we go home?" The instant a partner in a waltz brought me back to my seat: "Una, shall we go home?" Finally, to oblige him, we went home. It was only six o'clock when we left the ball-room.

Job. You went home at six o'clock to oblige him? Poor fellow!

Una. [*Starts up.*] Perhaps you think that's all?

Job. I hope so—for his sake.

Una. In the carriage—a scene. I made no answer. Arrived at home—a scene. I made no answer. This morning—another scene, in the course of which he threw up the window, pitched my beautiful dress away, and then flung himself out——

Job. and Mrs. J. [*Half rising.*] Flung himself out?

Una. —Out of the door.

Job. and Mrs J. [*Relieved, and reseating.*] Oh!

Mrs. J. I thought you meant he threw himself out of the window!

Una. No. He contented himself with throwing my dress out. Actually threw it out of the window. [*Getting near* JOB-LOTS.]

' *Ant.* · [*Down,* R. C.] I saw it wiz my own eyes. It is ze bare-faced truth.

Una. Antoinette, hold your tongue! [ANTOINETTE *goes back.*]

Job. [*Rising.*] It's a mere lover's quarrel. It'll blow over. [*Crosses to* MRS. JOBLOTS, *who rises.*]

Una. Blow over! You don't know me, papa, if you say that. Everything is over between Fred and me forever. I have made a solemn resolution.

Mrs. J. [*Nodding to* JOBLOTS.] Your father will see to it by-and-by.

Job. [*Winking at her.*] Yes, my dear.

Una. [L.] You know how good-tempered I invariably am. Well, this time I feel fully aroused. I will not go back to that brute again.

Mrs. J. [*Crosses to meet her.*] Come, my dear; you need a rest.

Una. Antoinette, another handkerchief. [*Fumbles in her pocket for one, while she hands the first to her maid.*] Oh, mamma —mamma! I feel so wretched. [*Takes handkerchief and Manual from the satchel which* ANTOINETTE *carries.*] There's your Manual. It isn't a bit of good. [JOBLOTS, *convulsed with laughter, drops on sofa.*]

Mrs. J. My dear, it tells you how to curb your temper.

Una. But it does'nt tell you how to curb your husband's temper—[*Crosses,* C.], and that's the main point.

Mrs. J. I'm sure, if you followed its instructions——

Una. [R. C.] Followed its instructions! [*Seizing book and turning over pages rapidly.*] Listen to this, papa: [*Reads.*] "No matter how you find your husband, always meet him with a smile." [*Speaks.*] Did you ever try that? Easy, isn't it? [*Turns over more pages, and then to* MRS. JOBLOTS.] "To husbands : Whatever you find your wife's mood to be advance to her frankly, and greet her with a smile." [*Speaks.*] Imagine two people as mad as fury—[*Clinching her fingers.*] and grinning—[*Illustrates it.*] at each other ! [*Throws book on the ground.*] I shall never smile again. [*Hysterically.*] That man has broken my heart. [*Sobbing.*]

Mrs. J. Come, my dear, and rest awhile. [*Taking her arm and leading her up stage.*]

Una. Mamma ! Papa ! [*Sobbing as she goes up.*] He has wrecked my whole life. [*Turning suddenly.*] Where is my poor little Beaucie ? [*Seeing him safe in* ANTOINETTE'S *arms, resumes her sobs.*] He is my only comfort. [*Exit,* R. *arch, with* MRS. JOBLOTS, *followed by* ANTOINETTE *and the dog.*]

Job. [*Sees the Manual on the floor, picks it up and flings it on the table.*] Hang the Manual ! That book's responsible for all the trouble. But it'll all come right. A few days' absence will heal the wound. [*Gets,* L.]

Sarah. [*Enters,* L. C., *announces.*] Mr. and Mrs. Naggitt. [JULIUS *and* RHODA *enter arm in arm,* L. C. *She quite smiling, he very stiff.* SARAH *exits,* L. C.]

Rho. Good-morning, papa !

Job. Why, good-morning, daughter ! . Good-morning, Julius !

Julius. [*Brings* RHODA *forward to a chair, seeing her seated politely, then, in the coldest possible tone.*] Good-morning, sir ! [RHODA *ceases smiling and looks at him.*]

Job. We have just heard nice things about your brother-in-law, Urquhart. [*To* RHODA.] Una has just arrived in tears.

Jul. Never mind all that for the present, if you please. Has Mrs. Joblots gone out ?

Job. [*Astonished.*] No ! [*Continues from this to stare at* JULIUS *in dumb amazement.*]

Jul. Will you have the extreme kindness to inform her of my presence ? [JOBLOTS *rings bell.* SARAH *enters,* L. C.]

Job. Ask your mistress to step here. [SARAH *exits,* R. *arch.*]

Rho. What is the matter, darling ?

Jul. You will find out soon enough, sweetest.

Mrs. Joblots. [*Re-entering with* SARAH, R. *arch.*] Ah ! Julius and Rhoda ! You are just in time. Only think—poor Una !

Jul. [*Pushing chair forward for* RHODA.] Will you kindly be seated, madam? [MRS. JOBLOTS *looks at him, wondering.*] Take a chair. [*Pause.*] Please ! [SARAH *exits,* L. C.]

Mrs. J. [*As she crosses,* R., *amazed.*] What in the name of——

Job. Yes—that's what I want to know—what in the name of——

2

Jul. Madam! Sir! [*The old couple look from one to the other in amazement.*]

Mrs. J., Job., Rho. Well, I——[*Half rising.*]

Jul. [*Silencing them with a gesture.*] If you please—[*They drop into seats simultaneously. He continues.*] it is now some eighteen months since I had the eccentric idea of asking you for the hand of your daughter——

Mrs. J. [*Half rising.*] Julius, this——

Jul. I beg you will let me continue. Your daughter—[*Looks at her.*] had then the appearance of extreme fragility and delicacy. But it was merely an appearance. She possessed then, and *now* possesses in a tenfold degree, since she has acquired her present robustness, a capacity for taking her own part equalled by few and excelled by none of her sex.

Rho. [*With an appealing gesture to* MR. *and* MRS. JOBLOTS.] I assure you I don't know what it's all about. He asked me to come here in the pleasantest manner, and now he breaks out in this way.

Jul. [L. C., *Curling the ends of his mustache.*] She was lovely then. She is lovely now. I don't deny it.

Job. Come to the point, sir.

Jul. I am coming to the point. Your daughter was a model young lady—*as a young lady*—bright, sociable, affectionate, and natural.

Mrs. J. [*Aside.*] She followed the Manual.

Jul. But when she became Mrs. Julius Naggitt, she vanished. The vanishing lady wasn't a circumstance to her. Where had the gentle, sociable, and affectionate creature gone?

Rho. [*Starts up snappishly.*] She had gone with you; that's what changed her.

Jul. Have I exaggerated? How is that for vinegar? [RHODA *seats herself with an angry look at him.*] I find—instead of the gentle, sociable, and affectionate young girl—an acrid, bitter, imperious woman, who has set out to make me miserable for life. I won't attempt to detail my sufferings, but I ask you if I don't deserve a better fate. Am I, or am I not, the kindest, gentlest, quietest, best fellow in the world—[*All give him a wondering look.*] bar none. [*All turn away.*] Well, she takes pleasure in thwarting my every wish. If I propose going out, she wants to stay at home. If she finds me set on a quiet evening at home, she insists on going out. If I won't go, she goes without me. If I form one opinion, she embraces another. [*To* JOBLOTS.] You don't know what it is, my dear sir—a wife who contradicts you incessantly. I've tried everything—firmness, gentleness, entreaties, threats. I even consulted a doctor. He advised cruelty—[*All start up.* Mrs. Joblots *embraces* Rhoda, *who rises.*] in small doses. He's a homœopath.

Mrs. J. [*Rises.*] Cruelty!

Jul. [*Producing a diary.*] This day-book, in which I have registered my charges against her, will tell you the whole story. I can't—its too long. [*Opens book.*]

Job. Do take off your hat.

Jul. [*Not heeding him.*] I'll open any page haphazard. Listen to this. [*Reads*]. "February 8th—a row because I said the first woman ruined the first man, and its been that way ever since."

Job. But *why* did you say so?

Jul. [*Not heeding, reads.*] "February 12th—cold veal for breakfast."

Mrs. J. [R., *To* Rhoda.] Why didn't you have it minced?

Rho. [*Calmly.*] He won't eat hash.

Jul. [*Reads.*] "I express my aversion to cold veal. I don't eat it. I won't eat it! February 14th, Valentine's Day—cold veal; out of spite I don't eat it. 15th, 16th, 17th—Cold veal I proceed to violence." [*All start.*] "I send it down and order it to be warmed."

Rho. Enough, sir. What do you expect to make by all this? What are you driving at?

Jul. [*Offers book to* Joblots.] I intrust these notes to you. After you have read them I intend to have them published, without names, of course—[Rhoda *gets to* Mrs. Joblots.] as a warning to all my friends who are contemplating matrimony. They shan't go it blind at all events.

Rho. Well, is that all?

Jul. [*Politely.*] No. [*To* Mr. *and* Mrs. Joblots.] I have long thought over a way to end this thing. At one time I contemplated the Brooklyn Bridge. But upon calmer reflections I adopted a plan with fewer inconveniences. I give you back your daughter.

Rho. What!

Mrs. J. What do you mean? ⎫ [*Nearly together.*]

Job. Julius, my son—— ⎭

Jul. Don't—don't recall that bitter relationship. Let us be friends, not enemies.

Mrs. J. [*Crosses to him.*] You can't do such a thing.

Jul. Who will prevent me?

Rho. [R.] The law, sir, for one thing.

Jul. [*Crosses to her.*] Do you know of any law which forbids my starting at this moment for parts unknown and remaining away for the next fifty years?

Rho. There must be, and I'll find it. [*Stage,* R.]

Jul. Do. [*To others, politely.*] I wish you a very good-morning. [*Looks around for his hat.*] Where is my hat?

Rho. This is too much!

Mrs. J. Are you actually unconscious that you have been standing in this room with your hat on ever since you entered it?

Jul. [*Takes it off.*] I beg ten thousand pardons. [*To* RHO-DA.] I'll have your trunks sent around at once.

Job. More baggage! They make my house a railway depot. [*Stage,* L.]

Rho. Depend upon it, I make you pay for this.

Jul. Excuse me! No, I shall pay for nothing from this time out. The bank is closed. [*Buttons his pockets.*] The bank is closed, and the cashier has evaporated. Ta! ta! [*Exits,* L. C.]

Job. [*As each looks at the other.*] Well, upon my word! It's unheard of. [*Seated,* L.]

Jenny. [*Runs in* R. 1 *door.*] What's the matter? [*Crosses to* JOBLOTS.]

Job. [*Rises.*] My dear, make four cups of tea.

Jenny. All right. [*Exits* R. U. D.]

Mrs. J. [*Crosses to* RHODA.] You are altogether in the wrong! Isn't she, Jeremiah? [RHODA *flounces up stage.*]

Job. Yes, dear. [MRS. JOBLOTS *gets,* R.]

Una. [*Enters* R. U. D.] Rhoda, you here? [*To others.*] What has happened?

Job. [*Advancing.*] Julius has brought her back. You may shake hands. Her husband wants no more of her. [RHODA *goes up.*] You want no more of yours. [*Crossing to* UNA.] It's the same thing arrived at in different ways.

Mrs. J. [R.] A wife owes her husband respect and obedience. Julius is not at all bad, as men go. Why exasperate the man, anyway?

Rho. You say this, mamma, you?

Mrs. J. Why not?

Rho. Why? Because I was applying your system.

Mrs. J. My system! [*Picks up Manual from the table and offers it to her.*] Show it to me in the Manual.

Rho. [*Crosses,* R., *takes book and throws it away.*] It wasn't your Manual, it was yourself.

Mrs. J. I!

Rho. Yes. Haven't you always led papa by the nose? [JOBLOTS *holds his nose and drops into a chair overcome with laughter, his back to the others.* MRS. JOBLOTS *looks at him and the others in open-mouthed wonder.*]

Mrs. J. Child!

Una. [L. C., *Crosses to her father.*] Yes, papa. You always did what mamma told you. I never saw you show a will of your own. [JOBLOTS *turns to face her squarely.*] "Yes, dear," that's all you ever had to say. "We won't do so and so." "Yes, dear." "We'll go here and there." "Yes, dear." "Mr. Urquhart will make an excellent husband for Una." "Yes, dear;" and that's where you made the greatest mistake of your life. Always "Yes, dear," and yet you've always been happy. How were we to know that other men were different?

Rho. [R. C.] That's so. And I said to myself, Mamma's system is the true secret of married happiness, and her system was to have everything her own way in everything. [*Up stage with* UNA.]

Job. [*Meets* MRS. JOBLOTS, C., *laughing.*] By Jove! it's the truth, my dear, though I never realized it before. What do you say? It seems to me I always did do as you told me.

Mrs. J. Because I always asked you to do what your own good sense approved in every case. [*To* RHODA.] But you merely tried your husband's patience to show off your authority.

Job. You didn't make him happy.

Una. It's a husband's duty to be happy.

Mrs. J. [*Crossing to* UNA.] Una, mind your own affairs. I'm speaking to your sister. But you, neither of you, even understood my system. It can only be applied by husbands and wives who love each other—better than themselves.

Job. [R. C.] Without that, no system will do anything.

Rho. [R.] Well, I confess I never looked at it from that point of view.

Job. [*Crosses to her, kindly taking her hand.*] Then go back home and tell your husband so.

Rho. I? Never! Acknowledge myself in the wrong? He would gloat over it. He would take every advantage.

Una. [L.] That he would. Don't you do it!

Job. [*Crosses to* UNA.] Una! You see, my dear—[*To* MRS. JOBLOTS.] the trouble is that, when young people promise at the altar nowadays to love each other they don't mean it. They mean to have a fine home, fine company, to have all they want, to get all they can, and to give nothing. They have too much—there's no room for love. Ah! when we married we had no horse and carriage, no furniture à la Louis quatorze, no bric-à-brac, no peach-blow, except that on your cheek, [*Pats her cheek.*] no curios worth twelve thousand dollars, no dresses worth twelve hundred, no dinners at fifty dollars a head. We'd have thought it a sin. [*Up stage a little and down,* R.]

Mrs. J.   [*Crosses to* UNA.]   Your father is right.

Job.   Yes, dear.

Una.   But, mamma, times have changed.

Job.   Not for the better. Look at your mother. When she married she could read, write, and cipher like a man. Her only weakness was her spelling. She did make mistakes sometimes. She does so still.

Mrs. J.   [L. C.]   Not as many as I used to.

Job.   No, dear. But what she did understand was the orthography of the heart.   [*Arm round her waist.*]

Mrs. J.   Thank you, dear.

Job.   These girls speak French. But can they wash a baby?

Una.   That's the nurse's business.

Job.   [*Crosses to* UNA.]   Your mother nursed all three of you.

Una.   Mother is stronger than I.

Job.   [*To* MRS. JOBLOTS.]   You've brought them up wrong. We have social queens instead of women, wives, and mothers. I'm to blame, too. As they grew up I was too vain of them. I sat open-mouthed while they talked to me like an encyclopædia all about the women of the eighteenth century. But what does it all amount to, when they can't live happily with a nineteenth-century man?   [*Crosses,* R.]   Love your husband—that's my system. Bring up your children. Keep the pot boiling, and don't bother about French, Dutch, or Hebrew, Abelard and Heloise, the Concord philosophy, or any of that stuff.

Una.   [*Starts up.*]   You want us to go back a hundred years?

Job.   [*To* UNA.]   No. I want you to go back five hundred years, six thousand years, when woman was man's rib, and, with all her faults—heaven bless her—stuck to him through thick and thin.   [*Arm around* MR. JOBLOTS' *waist.*]

Sarah.   [*Enters,* L. C., *and comes to* UNA.]   Please'm, Mr. Urquhart wants to see you.

Mrs. J.   [*Crosses to her.*]   Your husband—capital!

Una.   I'm not at home—stop. Say I'm not at home to him.

Sarah.   Yes'm.   [*Going.*]

Mrs. J.   [*Gets,* L., *to* SARAH.]   Sarah, wait. [*Down to* UNA.]

Sarah.   Yes'm.   [*Stops.*]

Mrs. J.   Una, I beg you will see your husband.

Una.   Mamma, it's out of the question. [MRS. JOBLOTS *flounces to* L.]

Rho.   She's right. Una, be a woman.

Job.   [*Down,* R., *to* UNA.]   Rhoda, hush.

Una.   [*To* SARAH.]   Not at home to him.

Sarah.   Yes'm.   [*Going.*]

Job. [*Crosses to* SARAH.] Sarah!

Sarah. Yes, sir.

Job. Hold on a bit. [SARAH *stops.*] Una, your old father begs you to receive your husband.

Una. [R. C., *After a struggle.*] It's very hard, papa, but I obey. [*To* SARAH.] Show him in. [*Gets to chair at table,* L.]

Sarah. Yes'm. [*Exit joyfully,* L. C.]

Mrs. J. [*Crosses to* JOBLOTS.] Let us leave them alone. [*Going.*]

Job. Yes, dear.

Rho. [*To* UNA.] Would you like me to stay?

Una. It's not necessary.

Job. [*At door.*] Rhoda!

Rho. Coming, papa! [*Exit with* MR. *and* MRS. JOBLOTS, R. arch.]

Una. [*Quite unconcernedly throws herself into a seat, down and picks up a book, trying to conceal her inner feelings, and failing, utters, half to herself:*] Oh, pshaw!

Urquhart. [*Enters, quickly and eagerly, trembling with controlled anger.*] Una [*Sees her, and comes down*], I left my office to go home and lunch with you. I was told that you had left with your trunks. What does it mean?

Una. [L.] It means that I have left you.

Urq. Come, Una, this is a joke.

Una. Do you think so? You'll soon find out differently.

Urq. What do you complain of in me?

Una. Oh, nothing—merely having made me miserable for the past two years—the time we've been married. That's all. You can't say I haven't had patience.

Urq. [*Puts hat on chair,* C.] I admit that I was a little hasty this morning.

Una. A little hasty! [*Crosses,* R.] It was a perfectly horrible scene. You threatened that you would never take me out into society again.

Urq. I don't want you to dance. I can't bear to see you in the arms of another man with indifference.

Una. In the arms of another man!

Urq. Yes—in the arms! Worse yet—your face near his, his breath almost touching your cheek.

Una. [R.] No!

Urq. I say yes. I know it. In the waltz especially.

Una. It goes so fast one doesn't have time to notice anything.

Urq. Doesn't he hold you round the waist and clasp your hand?

Una.   Who ?

Urq.   Who ?   The other man.

Una.   Our hands are gloved. So are my arms. I wear thirty-button gloves.

Urq.   You don't wear thirty-button waists.

Una.   [*Stage,* R.]   The fashion may come in.

Urq.   A pretty figure we cut, we husbands ; we dress up our wives and lead them round to these gentlemen that they may spin you about from midnight till six o'clock in the morning.   And what do we do ?

Una.   There's no harm in dancing.   We learn to dance at school.

Urq. .   Among children it is very pretty.   And quite moral.

Una.   Well, drop the parties.   There's the theatre.

Urq.   Well, I take you to the theatre.

Una.   Yes, once in two years.

Urq.   As often as there's a good play.

Una.   And then, instead of attending to the play, you are watching to see how many opera-glasses are turned on me.

Urq.   I can't understand how a well-bred man can ogle a respectable woman with whom he's not acquainted.

Una.   Well, he has to look at her first to find out whether he's acquainted with her, hasn't he ?   But so much for the theatre, if that were all.

Urq.   [L.]   Is there anything else ?

Una.   Yes, there is this : You get more and more unbearable every day.   I can't go out without being asked where I'm going, nor come home without being asked where I've been. You won't let me make calls—you won't let me receive calls. [*Crosses,* L.]

Urq.   Calls from gentlemen—certainly not.   Let these young bachelors call on the girls.

Una.   We can't lead a life of perpetual *tête-à-tête.*

Urq.   [*Approaching her.*]   I don't ask it.   I only ask not to be condemned to the white tie and swallow-tail five times a week.   I beg you not to pass your whole life outside your home, and not to make your house a rendezvous for every simpering ninny in town.

Una.   [*Sits.*]   You can have the house to yourself now, and receive whom you please.

Urq.   [*Up and down nervously.*]   Una, you are not in earnest. You are acting a part. You do love me. Remember how happy we have been. If you knew how your leaving me makes me suffer !

Una.   It's the last pain I shall give you—I promise you that ; I didn't marry to live like Bluebeard's wife. I love company.

Urq. And I love only you [*down to her*], think of you, live for you only. The smile you give a stranger seems stolen, to me.

Una. A little while ago I was not to dance ; now I'm not even to smile. To-morrow you'll ask me to go out veiled. [*Crosses,* R.] The woman who invented veils must have been hideously ugly.

Urq. Why do you delight to torment me?

Una. Why do you delight to torment *me?*

Urq. [*Uncontrollable outburst.*] Oh, if I had known——

Una. Known what? That a wife can't be caged like a bird. Why, it was in society we met ! At a German ! You waltzed beautifully ! [*He advances to her.*] I lost a good partner when I married you—and got a poor husband. [*Laughing.*]

Urq. [*Turning away.*] You are wrong to jest on serious subjects.

Una. [R.] The most serious thing I know is to live a life exposed to your unmanly violence. [URQUHART *makes a movement.*] Yes—your unmanly violence ! This morning it was my dress out of the window—to-morrow it may be me. If you wanted a house-keeper for a wife, you ought to have advertised for a middle-aged, plain person, unaccustomed to society. I warn you that I shall never settle down to spend three hundred and sixty-five nights every year at home with you and cribbage— not even when I am sixty and wear glasses. [*Crosses,* L.]

Urq. Very well, madam ; since you treat me in this tone— enough of entreaty. You refuse to return home?

Una. I do. [*He turns up stage, gets hat, looks back.*]

Urq. A second time—you refuse to return ?

Una. Consider it refused for the third and last time.

Urq. Very well. I warn you that unless you come home to-day you never shall.

Una. I warn you that I never will.

Urq. You are satisfied ?

Una. Perfectly.

Urq. Then the responsibility of everything that happens rests with you.

Una. Very good.

Urq. Good-morning.

Una. Good-morning. [URQUHART *exits.*] I said good-morning. [*Looks around, and is amazed to find herself alone.*] Gone ! He'll come back. [RHODA *and* MRS. JOBLOTS *enter,* R. *arch.*]

Mrs. Joblots. Well?

Una. It's settled. I stay here.

Mrs. J. You are mad.

Rhoda. [R.] She is right. [*Up and down,* C.]

Mrs. J. [*Snappy.*] Hold your tongue.

Joblots. [*Entering.*] Well?

Mrs. J. She's let him go.

Job. [*Crosses to* UNA.] You wish to make your father and mother miserable!

Jenny. [*Enters,* R. U. D.] Are you going to stay to dinner?

Job. Jenny, make another cup of tea.

Jenny. Why, mamma?

Mrs. J. My poor child, your two sisters have returned home to us. Una has left Frederick, and as for Rhoda, Julius has left her.

Jenny. How could you!

Rho. Silence, miss.

Una. Your turn 'll come.

Hoffman. [*Enters,* L. C., *with a bouquet.*] Ladies, good-morning. [*To* JENNY.] Permit me. [*Offers bouquet.*]

Jenny. [*Waving him away.*] No, thank you.

Hoff. Why not?

Jenny. [*Taking ring from finger.*] Here's your engagement ring.

Hoff. But, Jenny——

Mrs. J. Jenny, what are you doing?

Jenny. If my sisters have come home after such a short experience of marriage, I'd better stay where I am. Charles, you are free. [*Crosses to* RHODA.]

Una. [*To* JOBLOTS.] She only takes things in time.

Mrs. J. Una!

Job. [R. C.] You refuse to marry the doctor?

Jenny. I can't marry at the very moment my sisters are getting unmarried. [SARAH *enters with tray; crosses to table,* L.]

Hoff. But, Jenny, darling——

Jenny. [*Crosses,* C., *waving him off.*] You men are all alike. [*Up to table to serve tea.*]

Sarah. Here's the tea.

Mrs. J. [*To* JOBLOTS.] What am I to do?

Job. [*Handing her the book.*] Consult the Manual! [UNA *and* RHODA *take a cup each.* JENNY *serves sugar as* SARAH *places tray on table.* MRS. JOBLOTS *sinks on chair.* JOBLOTS *laughs.* HOFFMAN *dashes bouquet to floor.*]

QUICK CURTAIN.

ACT II.

SCENE.—*Drawing-Room at Urquhart's, elegantly furnished in the best modern style, in contrast to the old-fashioned interior of Act I. Piano at* L. C. *Immense ferns in* C., *with sofa between them. An elaborate mantel at* R. *Doors* C., R., *and* L., *up stage.*

SCHLAGG, *a German-American valet discovered with a small watering-pot and a sponge watering the ferns and wiping off the leaves. Very large feather duster under his arm.*

Schlagg. I guess it was a break up for goot dis times. Missus, she vont come backs any more and de governor is down in de mouf. I vas down in de mouf myself. It vould be all de same, as for me, but for one thing; my vife is my missusses woman, and ven my missus goes her off, my vife she go too mit her. Dat makes us both down in de mouf in dis house—and by gracious it vos vorse mit me—for I am merried only dese three months.

Julius. [*Enters,* C.] Mr. Urquhart in, John? [*Down,* L.]

Schl. Yes, sir, he vos in his room! [*Hesitates about going.*] [JULIUS *sits,* C., *and takes up a newspaper.*] If you please, sir, may I beg de favor of an answer to von leedle question?

Jul. [*Looking over paper.*] You may, John.

Schl. Do you happen to know if dis state of tings is going to last a long time some more?

Jul. What business is that of yours?

Schl. I know it seems not of my business, but my whole happiness is dere already.

Jul. I don't understand. [*Putting paper down.*]

Schl. No, sir—nobody never understand de troubles of oder peoples. My vife has gone off mit Mrs. Urquhart, and she stay off—dot is two weeks now.

Jul. Well, can't you go and see her? [*Seated,* L. *of sofa.*]

Schl. Yes—but vat is dat? Twice a veek in de front airy, in de dark—vit de post-office man going by all de time. And de more I don' see her—de more I loves her all de while. I can't help it. By gracious me, none of us can help it. [*Sits confidentially by* JULIUS.] Ve are men. Ve are all of us dat vay.

Jul. [*First indignant at the familiarity, then rising, smiling.*] Speak for yourself. [*Stage,* R.]

Schl. [*Rising.*] Dat vos so. I am merried only three months, and my vife she is merried de same length of time. It is our honeymoons—it vas not a very full moons eider. But dere is a vay to fix. If Mr. Urquhart vill not take back his vife—vy he not take back mine? [*Dusts* JULIUS' *clothes familiarly with his feather duster.*]

Jul. [*Giving him a look and a push.*] Speak to *him* about it. [*Crosses,* L.]

Schl. As soon I would blow off a barrel of gunpowder as talk it to him.

Jul. Really?

Schl. [*Dusting him.*] He feels too bad of it. I must gonsider his feelings. I owe him forty dollars vorth of gonsideration a month.

Jul. [*Giving him a bank-note.*] Do you? Now you owe my feelings some consideration. Drop the subject and announce me.

Schl. [*Pockets the money, folding it and placing it in his vest.*] Thank you, sir. But it vas a grade pity dis Franco-German alliance of ours don't get a fair chance. [*Going.*] Ah! Autoinette! Antoinette! I love you so. Ach. [*Exit,* L. *door.*]

Jul. [*Getting* R.] There's no doubt about it. Fred takes the separation hard. If I could think of a good way to bring him and his wife together, I'd do it. As for myself, I'm happy. I've given up our flat, stored the furniture, and taken bachelor apartments in the "Benedick."

Urquhart. [*Enters gloomily,* L. D.] Morning, Julius. What do you want? [*Throws himself into a seat,* L. C.]

Jul. Finding you had not been down town to-day, I called to see if you were ill.

Urq. Why should I be ill?

Jul. [*Sits,* C.] Don't get angry.

Urq. I'm not angry.

Jul. How did you enjoy yourself last night?

Urq. Last night? Where?

Jul. Why, at the Kermess. Don't you recollect going? I said, "Let's have a good time;" you said, "You didn't feel like it." So we went.

Urq. I didn't notice where we were; looked at the dancing. [*Shrugs his shoulders.*] Not much!

Jul. I looked at the girls. [*Shrug.*] Not much!

Urq. [*Shrug.*] Not much in anything!

Jul. [*Shrug.*] Not much! [*A pause. Mutual crossing.*

URQUHART *picks up paper.* JULIUS *picks up a book.*] Only to think ; it's two weeks to-day.

Urq. Beg pardon ?

Jul. It's two weeks to-day since we were bachelors again. It was on the 25th, you remember ?

Urq. Do you keep count ? [*With a sneer.*]

Jul. A date is not a regret. I do keep count ; but I do it cheerfully. [*Counts on fingers.*] 26th, 27th, 28th—

Urq. I simply banish the whole thing.

Jul. So you don't love Una ?

Urq. I detest her.

Jul. Can one forget so soon ? You certainly adored each other once.

Urq. [*Pettishly, rising and tossing paper aside.*] Adored !

Jul. Yes, adored. You kissed each other before people.

Urq. [*Astonished.*] Before people ?

Jul. [*Rises.*] Yes, before Rhoda and me. Folks used to say : " They are charming—there's a couple won't get tired of each other."

Urq. What's the use of recalling all that when everything's over ? [*Crosses*, L.]

Jul. Are you sure everything is over ? [URQUHART, *with an impatient movement, throws himself into a chair.*] I say, are you going to resume your bachelor life again ?

Urq. Certainly.

Jul. Go about and act as if you were free ?

Urq. Unquestionably.

Jul. Keep bachelor hall ?

Urq. Yes.

Jul. Where ?

Urq. Here.

Jul. What ! Have the boys in here among the household gods?

Urq. Since the household goddess deserts it, certainly. [*Rises.*]

Jul. They'll break things.

Urq. [*Crosses*, R.] One break more or less won't signify.

Schlagg. [*Enters, c., very frisky.*] If you vas please, sir, my vife is here.

Urq. Well, what is that to us ?

Schl. [*Aside.*] How selfish dey is. [*Aloud.*] If you please, sir, she wants to see you.

Jul. [*Crosses to* URQUHART. *Aside.*] Aha ! She brings a flag of truce. [*To* SCHLAGG, *after seeing that* URQUHART *remains silent.*] Show your wife in. [SCHLAGG *exit quite fris-*

kily.] I'm rather curious to hear what message your wife sends you. My wife don't send me any.

Schl. [*Announcing at* c.] Frau Antoinette von Koppel-meisterlachverstangenfellen Schlagg.

Jul. [*To* URQUHART.] He is announcing his wife. Show her in, John. [*Crosses,* L.]

Antoinette. [*Enters,* c.] *Bonjour*, gentlemens. [*Her air is polite, but independent.*]

Jul. How do you do, Antoinette?

Ant. [c.] Zank you, monsieur, and ze gentlemen—zay quite well?

Jul. [*Crosses,* c.] Well and happy, as you perceive. [*Aside to* URQUHART.] Don't look so miserable. [*Up and down,* R.]

Urq. [c.] [*To* ANTOINETTE.] What do you wish?

Ant. [L.] When madam depart, she had only ze time to take away ze most necessaire articles. Her costumes for ze ball, and ze toilettes for ze reception. She have all leave behind, and if monsieur haf no objection, I am come por zem especially to fetch zem away, *voilà tout.*

Urq. [*To* JULIUS, *indignantly.*] Her ball dresses!

Jul. [R.] I sent Rhoda everything. Why preserve the frame when the picture is gone? I thought I had a masterpiece—it turned out a poor copy, and I got rid of it. [*Stage,* R.]

Ant. Shall I have monsieur's permission to take away ze costumes of madame?

Urq. Why does my wife send for her ball dresses in our present situation?

Ant. Vy, for what but to go to ze balls, monsieur! *Voilà! c'est tout!*

Urq. [*To* JULIUS.] You hear that?

Jul. What does it matter? She has a perfect right. [*Crosses to* ANTOINETTE.] So the ladies are happy?

Ant. Oui, monsieur, especially ze wife of monsieur. [*Smiles at* JULIUS.] Madame is merry as a cricket all ze day, and sing like a bird all ze time. [*Goes up.*]

Jul. She never had her wings clipped. [*Crosses,* R.]

Urq. [*To* SCHLAGG, *who has been gazing in rapture at his wife, and is now leaning over the piano grinning at her.*] What are you waiting for?

Schl. I'm looking at my vife.

Urq. Get out! [SCHLAGG *bounds out, throwing kisses at* ANTOINETTE, *who is imperturbable, and reappears instantly at another door.* R. U. E.]

Jul. Let him look. It's little enough. [*Crosses to* ANTOINETTE.] How do the ladies pass their time, Antoinette?

Urq. What do you want to know that for ?

Jul. No harm in it, and besides, it's no more than ordinary politeness to ask after a family we used to visit.

Ant. [L.] Zay get's up very early in zat house. Ze old lady gets up at seven o'clock, ze old monsieur he get up at eight, and so does Mademoiselle Jenny.

Jul. Ah! Miss Jenny! How about her marriage?

Ant. It's all smash—go up in a balloon—what you call it— broke off.

Jul. Broke off in a balloon, eh ?

Ant. She declare she vill not marry while zat her sisters and dere husbands separate.

Jul. Poor girl! She'll be single a long while.

Ant. [*Coldly.*] So her sisters tell to her. [JULIUS *coughs, crosses,* L.] Madame Naggitt and Madame Urquhart zay break-fast every morning at eleven o'clock.

Urq. Zay take it easy.

Ant. Zay are out so late effry night. [JULIUS *and* URQUHART *evince feeling.*]

Urq. So zay are out every night ? Where ?

Ant. To ze theatre. To ze opera. Dey went to ze races yesterday.

Urq. [*Crosses to* JULIUS.] Went to the races, and I hadn't the heart to !

Jul. Well, if they enjoy it——

Ant. At three o'clock ze ladies zay dress for a drive, or ze shopping ; Tuesdays and Fridays zay receive company—a great deal of company.

Urq. And, pray, what do they say to their guests?

Ant. [*Shrugs.*] I am not a guest. I do not know.

Urq. I mean, how do they explain our situation ?

Jul. [L.] Yes, I'm curious to hear that.

Ant. [*Crosses,* c.] Zay only state ze facts as zay oc-curred.

Urq. That's fortunate. [*Irritated tone.*]

Jul. Very fair.

Ant. Zat Monsieur Urquhart was always quarrelling viz madame.

Jul. One for you !

Ant. And zat Monsieur Naggitt had ze cruelty to send his vifes back to her parents for her to eat ze cold veal.

Urq. That's one for you !

Jul. You are right—one for me.

Urq. [*Crosses,* c.] The court will appreciate all this.

Jul. The court?

Urq. [*In a rage.*] I shall have a divorce. [*To* ANTOINETTE.] You may tell your mistress so, from me.

Ant. [R.] Bien, m'sieu'. I will take ze message. May I take ze costumes aussi?

Urq. Take anything you like. [*Crosses,* R.]

Ant. Merci, m'sieu'! I thank monsieur for his affability. Gentlemens, I have ze honor! [*Bows profoundly, goes up and meets* SCHLAGG, *who hugs her to confusion.*]

Schl. Mein Lieben! I'll help you! I'll help you! [*Puts his arm about her waist, they exeunt,* C. R.]

Jul. [*Aside.*] He's the happiest of us three.

Urq. [*Pacing up and down.*] They go to the races! They have reception days!

Jul. [L.] Wouldn't we? Come, they are having their good time, we'll have ours. [*Goes to piano, opens it.*] We'll be as jolly as they. Life's a burlesque, the world's a casino. Come, let's rehearse our parts in the farce. [*Sings and plays from* "*Josephine.*"] Eugene, Eugene, etc.

Urq. Stop that infernal racket.

Jul. [*Rises.*] Racket! We must live on racket now. Come! Be as jolly as I am. [*Drags him to piano.*] You can play better than I can. Give us a rousing chorus to warm up. [URQUHART *sits dejectedly, but does not play.*]

Schlagg. [*Enters and announces.*] Mr. and Mrs. Joblots. [JULIUS *and* URQUHART *start up.* SCHLAGG *exits.*]

Jul. You hear? [URQUHART *suddenly turns and begins to play. Both join in the chorus as before from* "*Josephine.*"] Eugene, Eugene, etc. [MR. *and* MRS. JOBLOTS *enter and stand in doorway,* C., *stupefied, while* JULIUS *begins to dance,* URQUHART *to play more boisterously, both as if unconscious of the presence of the old couple.*]

Joblots. [*As the young men turn around and subside.*] You are merry!

Jul. [*Seizes his hand.*] Ah! my dear sir! My dear Mrs. Joblots! [*Crosses to her.*]

Mrs. Joblots. [L. C., *To* URQUHART.] You are quite musical!

Urq. I piano a little bit.

Mrs. J. [*To* JOBLOTS.] He never played for us.

Jul. [R., *As* JOBLOTS *coughs.*] We men are so bashful. All brokers are that way.

Urq. Pray be seated.

Job. Excuse us for interrupting your little concert. [*He and* MRS. JOBLOTS *sit,* C., JULIUS *and* URQUHART *stand each side of them.*]

Mrs. J. [*To* JULIUS.] We intended to go to your house after our call on Frederick, but as we are all met together——

Job. We'll kill two birds with one stone.

Jul. To what are we indebted for the honor of this visit?

Mrs. J. Julius, you know that we have been expecting you every day for two weeks?

Jul. Where?

Job. At our house.

Jul. For what purpose?

Job. Come now, you know that this state of thing can't last.

Urq. So *we* think.

Job. Now, now, my dear boys, you know that Una and Rhoda are only children.

Urq. You should have brought them up to be women.

Job. This is hard for a father.

Mrs. J. [*Weeping.*] And for a mother. [*Rises to* JULIUS *and* URQUHART.] What have I ever done to you?

Urq. My dear Mrs. Joblots, I could live with you all my life; that is the highest compliment one can pay to a mother-in-law; but with my wife, never! [*Gets,* L.]

Jul. Existence with you, Mrs. Joblots, would be happiness. A son-in-law can say no fairer; but with your eldest daughter, excuse me—[*She moves.*] Don't insist. You will oblige me by not attempting it. [*Going to door,* L.] Frederick!

Urq. [*Joins him and takes his arm.*] Julius! [*To* MR. *and* MRS. JOBLOTS, *bowing in unison.*] We have the honor.

Jul. We have the honor. [*Both exeunt,* L. D., *with an air of mild dignity, arm in arm.*]

Mrs. J. [*Following up to door,* L.] They talk that way about your daughters, and you sit there as indifferent and cold——

Job. No, my dear, not cold, but trying to keep cool. [*Stage,* R.]

Schlagg. [*Announcing,* C.] Mrs. Naggitt and Mrs.—— [UNA *and* RHODA *enter, pushing past him, and he exits indignantly.*]

Mrs. J. Una! Rhoda! Heaven be praised you are here.

Una. [*Pausing, surprised.*] Mamma!

Rho. [*Same.*] Papa!

Una. You here? [*Looks from one to the other.*]

Job. On business.

Una. So am I. We have just heard something that makes us supremely happy.

Rho. Overjoyed!

Mrs. J. [*Crosses*, L. C.] You wouldn't be if you had heard what we did—that your husband wants a divorce.

Una. Antoinette has just told us. [*Crosses*, L. C.]

Mrs. J. And that makes you happy?

Una. Rapturous! I came at once to arrange particulars with Mr. Urquhart.

Rho. [L.] And I came to stand by her.

Mrs. J. This is unheard of.

Rho. [*Crosses*, C., *to* JOBLOTS.] How are your amiable sons-in-law?

Job. When we came in they were having a little song and dance.

Mrs. J. They were rioting and revelling. [JULIUS *enters,* L. D., *with a package of securities and remains unperceived.*]

Job. [*To* RHODA.] Your husband sings false.

Rho. [*Coldly.*] Then he sings as he talks.

Jul. [C.] Thank you. [*All turn slightly.*]

Rho. I'm not speaking to you. I came with my sister.

Jul. [*Critically, as if to himself.*] My late wife has grown decidedly stouter. [RHODA *turns up stage. To* UNA.] How do you do, Una?

Una. [L.] Well, I declare! What insolence!

Jul. [*Smiling, hands package in his hand to* JOBLOTS.] There, sir!

Job. What's this? [RHODA, *down*, L. C.]

Jul. The dowry Frederick and I received with your daughters. We can't send back the wives and keep the money —that wouldn't be fair.

Job. [R. C., *Taking it.*] I'm much obliged. I'll write a receipt, and add a certificate of honesty. [*Up with* MRS. JOB-LOTS.]

Jul. No need of receipt. You won't ask the money twice. [*Up.*]

Una. [*Aside to* RHODA.] It's all bluster. They're whistling to keep their courage up. [*Touches bell.*]

Rho. [*Same.*] They don't mean a word.

Job. [*To* MRS. JOBLOTS, *giving her the money.*] You take this, and don't lose it.

Jul. [*To* UNA *and* RHODA.] Is there anything I can do for you, ladies? [SCHLAGG *enters.*]

Una. [*Crosses to* SCHLAGG.] Will you ask Mr. Urquhart whether he can spare the time from his revelries to see me?

Schlagg. Yes, ma'm! He vill be glad. [*Exit* L. *door.*]

Jul. [*Aside.*] Is she weakening?

Mrs. J. [R, *Aside to* JOBLOTS.] Shall we stay?

Job. [*Aside to her.*] Let us wait in Una's room.

Mrs. J. [*Goes with* JOBLOTS *to door,* R., *and turns when about to exit.*] My dear child, let me beg you to reflect. You are partly to blame.

Una. But, mamma! If I am entirely satisfied!

Mrs. J. Your father and I are not.

Una. You'll get used to it in time, as I have. [*Crosses to desk,* R.]

Rho. As *we* have.

Job. [*Hopelessly.*] Come, dear. [*Going.*] Don't drop the money. [*Exeunt,* R. D.]

Rho. [*To* UNA, *but intending* JULIUS *to hear.*] You are fortunate. I only wish my little monster would ask for a divorce!

Jul. [*Sinks in chair,* L., *and stretches his legs, addressing the front.*] How happy I am these days—no cares, no house, no hours, no jaw. [RHODA *sits spitefully.*] I breakfast at the café, dine at the club, and give no account of my time to any Paul Pry, male or female.

Rho. Sir!

Jul. I am not speaking to you—I am addressing space.

Rho. [*To* UNA.] If I had known I would meet my—[*Checks herself.*] that I should meet a stranger here, I would not have come.

Una. [*Seated,* R.] Rhoda, be calm.

Rho. [*Going to her.*] You are right. I will be calm and indifferent. Oh! how could papa and mamma have been so mistaken! [*Going back to sofa, sits.*] They said: "He is much older than you, Rhoda, and, of course, not handsome, but he is a perfect gentleman." And a year afterward this perfect gentleman sets me down at their front door as he'd shoot a load of coal on the sidewalk.

Una. You had ceased to fascinate the Sultan.

Jul. [*As before.*] What a fool I was. Instead of being resolute from the start, I was affable and yielding. I look upon those eighteen months as a horrid dream. Thank goodness, I wake happy.

Rho. [*Approaching him.*] I suppose you consider that polite?

Jul. [*As before.*] Excuse me, I was addressing somebody in vacancy.

Rho. [*Turns to him spitefully.*] There's nobody in vacancy. But, be careful, my gentleman, or you'll get a good slap from vacancy. [*Crosses,* R. *Enter* URQUHART.]

Jul. [*As before.*] That's my wife.

Una. [*Sees* URQUHART, *rises.*] Here's the other. [URQU-
HART *bows calmly.*]

Urquhart. Ladies! [*To* RHODA.] How do you do, Rhoda?

Rho. [*Coldly.*] Good-morning!

Jul. [*Aside.*] He'll catch it.

Urq. [*Sarcastically to* RHODA.] How cold! [*Advances to
her.*]

Rho. [R. C.] I am not more so than I ought to be toward my sister's executioner.

Jul. Don't go too close. She came near biting *me*. [RHODA
flounces up stage.]

Urq. [*To* UNA.] You sent for me. I am at your service.

Una. If I am correctly informed, you are contemplating a
divorce?

Urq. [*Bringing chair forward.*] I am. Will you be seated?
[*Points to sofa.*]

Una. [*Sits*, C.] If agreeable to you that will be our topic.
[URQUHART *bows.*] I think with you that an absolute divorce is
better than a mere separation, which would compel me to bear,
or rather to endure, your name.

Jul. [*To* URQUHART, *who strives to hide an outburst.*] Keep
cool. I'll takes notes of this. [*Takes out a note-book and
writes.*] "Endure your name."

Una. After the divorce you can resume your bachelor life,
while I regain the advantages of a young girl.

Jul. [L., *Writes.*] "Young girl." [*Speaks.*] Perhaps!
[MR. *and* MRS. JOBLOTS *appear at* R. *door.*]

Urq. Be as brief as you can, please.

Una. I desire to be brief. [MR. *and* MRS. JOBLOTS *are seen
listening.*]

Joblots. [*Aside.*] They may be going to make it up.

Una. Then that point is settled. We shall have a divorce.
[MR. *and* MRS. JOBLOTS *disappear and close the door.*]

Jul. [*Closes the book.*] I should like to know what grounds
you two have.

Una. Grounds!

Jul. Yes; grounds for a divorce.

Una. Cruelty.

Jul. [*To* URQUHART.] I didn't know there was cruelty!

Urq. Neither did I.

Una. Throwing my dress out of the window.

Urq. You were not in it.

Una. [*To* RHODA.] He regrets that I was not in it.

Rho. I'll make a note of that. [*Gets out note-book and
writes same business as* JULIUS.] "Regrets she was not in it."

Jul. You can't get a divorce for that.

Una. The court will decide.

Jul. You can't get a lawyer to take such a case as that. Some shyster may, but a respectable member of the bar— never! [MR. *and* MRS. JOBLOTS *reappear,* R. *door.*]

Una. If that's not sufficient, I shall accuse him of insulting my mother and inflicting a painful wound upon her forehead.

Urq. I did?

Una. Yes, you. The occasion was a Sunday when I dined with my parents. My dear mamma, always thoughtful and considerate, had pressed you to take the supreme of a partridge. My darling papa, always obliging and full of tact, had produced some choice Lafitte from the cellar.

Joblots. [*Up stage,* R., *aside.*] Five dollars a bottle.

Una. You meanwhile were eating your wing and devouring the other with your eyes, when I took it.

Urq. I can't see the least harm in that.

Jul. Nor I.

Una. Wait. After dinner my sweet mamma offered you most delicately a few tickets for our church fair at a dollar each, whereupon, without the slightest cause, you answered roughly, "You've been sticking me with tickets for your church fairs long enough." My poor mother, trembling like a leaf, murmured : "I'm not compelling you to take them." "Yes, you are," says my gentleman, and at the same moment bringing his fist down on the table with a bang, that sent a pile of plates dancing in the air, a piece of one of them striking my darling mamma on the forehead. [*With great emotion.*] She was obliged to remain in bed for three weeks with a bandage over one eye.

Rho. [*Writing.*] "One month—bandage over both eyes."

Job. [*Aside to* MRS. JOBLOTS.] I don't remember that!

Mrs. Joblots. Neither do I! [*Both disappear.*]

Urq. [*Rises.*] There's not a syllable of truth in the whole tale.

Una. I know it. [*Rises.*] But you want a divorce and you want grounds. Ain't you much obliged to me for inventing such a good story?

Urq. But such a piece of brutality!

Una. Do you want a divorce?

Urq. I do, but I want a divorce with honor—something that leaves me with a shred of reputation, at least.

Una. Well, you may admit then that you merely insulted mamma.

Jul. You can't refuse her that. After all, it's only your mother-in-law.

Urq. No. There's a simpler way.

Una. Simpler than mine? Impossible!

Urq. Quite possible. When a husband and wife can't live together——

Una. As in *our* case.

Urq. I was about to add that! Besides, an absolute divorce can be procured for one cause only, the *flagrante delictu.*

Una. What's that?

Urq. I elope with someone or another.

Una. You would, would you? [*Furious.*] You dare to tell me to my face——[Rhoda *approaches her.*]

Urq. You must listen quietly, or I won't be divorced.

Una. [*Suppressing her anger.*] Oh, go on. I'm listening. [Mr. *and* Mrs. Joblots *reappear at door,* R.]

Mrs. Joblots. [*Aside.*] Are they making up?

Joblots. [*Aside.*] I think not, my dear.

Urq. Your plan makes me a ruffian, while mine is quite *à la mode.*

Una and Rhoda. À *la mode?*

Jul. [L.] Quite *à la mode.* Such husbands as do not elope, would like to.

Job. [*To his wife.*] Don't believe him, dear. [*Both disappear.*]

Una. [*To* Julius.] Speak for yourself.

Urq. You must not lose sight of the fact that there will be only a pretended elopement in our case. [*Crosses,* L. *He and* Rhoda *go up stage.*]

Jul. [*Meeting* Rhoda, C.] That's so, and if Rhoda doesn't mind either, why——

Rho. Rhoda! Of whom are you speaking?

Jul. Of you. If you are satisfied, we'll all of us be divorced in the same way—a four-cornered divorce.

Una. [*Down,* R., *to* Rhoda.] How amusing he is.

Urq. [*To* Una.] Your decision, if you please?

Una. [*Meets him.*] I say insults and cruelty. [*Stage,* R.]

Urq. I say an elopement. [*Stage,* L. Julius *and* Rhoda *meet,* C., *and turn up stage.* Una *and* Urquhart *meet,* C.]

Una. You will receive a summons in due time.

Urq. [*Stage,* L. H.] With pleasure.

Rho. [*To* Julius.] And you too.

Jul. I shall be delighted!

Una. I'll go to a lawyer at once.

Rho. And I'll go with you. [MR. *and* MRS. JOBLOTS *enter* R. *door.*]

Joblots. Stop! Your father forbids you to stir a step in this matter.

Mrs. Joblots. You will kill your mother.

Jul. [*To* MRS. JOBLOTS.] It must be done. [*Stage,* L.]

Mrs. J. [*Alarmed.*] Oh!

Urq. He means the divorce must be got.

Una. And he's quite right.

Job. You will not give up this wicked scheme?

Una. I'd die first.

Job. Then never enter my house again.

Mrs. J. Jeremiah!

Job. No, my dear. She shall never put her foot in our house.

Jul. Bravo!

Una. [*To* RHODA.] We'll go to a hotel, that's all.

Job. Go! but understand, I will not support you.

Una. [*Half-crying.*] You will not?

Job. And you haven't a cent.

Rho. [*Crosses to* JOBLOTS.] We have our dowry.

Job. No, no! No marriage, no dowry.

Una. We'll sell our diamonds.

Rho. And after that we'll starve.

Mrs. J. [*To* JOBLOTS.] You go too far.

Job. No, my dear. Good-morning, ladies!

Una. [*Crosses to* JOBLOTS.] But, papa!

Job. There's no more papa.

Rho. [*Crosses to* MRS. JOBLOTS.] Mamma! [*In tears.*]

Mrs. J. There's still a mamma! [*Opens her arms.* JOBLOTS *whirls her round.*]

Job. Come, no weakness now.

Mrs. J. A mother is not a father.

Job. No, I don't say she is! [*Both girls sob.*] But come, come. Let's go. [*Aside, much moved.*] Or hang it, I shall hug 'em too! [*Hurries* MRS. JOBLOTS *off,* C. L. UNA *sobs,* RHODA *weeps,* URQUHART *and* JULIUS *exchange glances.*]

Jul. [L.] The old gentleman was grand. I'll send him a congratulatory card.

Una. [*Drying her eyes.*] Crying won't mend matters. Come, Rhoda.

Rho. Where?

Una. Wherever you like.

Rho. I came away without my pocket-book.

Una. Never mind. I have mine. [*Produces and opens it.*] I have four dollars and a postage-stamp.

Rho. We'll use the stamp to inform mamma where we are stopping. She won't see us want.

Una. [*Crosses,* c.] Let's go, then. [*They are going up.* URQUHART *meets and stops them.*]

Urq. Pardon me, ladies!

Una. [*Stops suddenly,* c.] What is it?

Urq. [L. C.] Behind the injured husband still remains the gentleman. The latter now addresses you.

Jul. [L.] What's he up to now? [*Sits at piano and plays softly.*]

Urq. [*To ladies.*] You are not divorced yet.

Una. Unfortunately.

Urq. Unfortunately! So it would be discourteous to leave you without a shelter.

Una. There *are* hotels.

Rho. And our mother.

Jul. Certainly, there *are* both.

Urq. [*To* JULIUS.] Let the gentleman still speak. [*To ladies.*] Stop here.

Una. Here? Never!

Urq. [*To* JULIUS.] You see!

Jul. [*To* URQUHART.] Let me try them. [*Crosses to the ladies.*] Permit us to offer you that room—[*Indicating room on* R.] for the present. As for Fred, he will come with me. You will be alone.

Rho. [R.] On that understanding we accept.

Una. It is understood that we *pay* for the room?

Jul. We wouldn't think of it.

Una. [*Severely.*] Then, upon what terms?

Jul. Perfect strangers, but guests. If that don't suit—pay. At all events, make yourselves at home. Come, Fred.

Urq. [*Looking at* UNA, *aside.*] She's marble. [*Crosses past* JULIUS.]

Una. [*Looking at* URQUHART, *aside.*] He's adamant.

Jul. [*Same, looking at* RHODA.] She has certainly grown decidedly stouter. [*Exits with* URQUHART, L. *door.*]

Rho. At all events, we'll soon be free.

Una. [*Mournfully.*] Do you know a lawyer? [*Crosses,* L.]

Rho. No; but we'll look in the papers. The thing that puzzles me is what we'll say to him. My Julius was right. There's not the least ground for *you.* If your husband only *would* elope with somebody else. [*Both sit,* c.]

Una. [*Exulting.*] He won't. He loves me too much.

Rho. I didn't quite like his proposing it.

Una. It was only to oblige me.

Rho. But I don't like the idea of his thoughts running in that direction.

Una. You positively terrify me. Oh, no, he wouldn't be so base.

Rho. We must be prepared for anything.

Una. It's so horrible to think of.

Rho. Then you love him still?

Una. No; I don't love him. But I'm jealous all the same!

Rho. You were wild for a divorce just now.

Una. I thought he would give in.

Rho. The case is plain—you love him madly. Go and beg him to forgive you. [*Rises.*]

Una. [*Rises.*] Don't talk nonsense to me. Your husband is right. You are most exasperating.

Rho. [R.] Exasperating, when I advise you to make up with your husband? I like that.

Una. You only do it to provoke me.

Rho. You'd provoke a saint! [*Exits angrily, R. door.*]

Una. [*Alone.*] Can Frederick really harbor a false thought? Could he be so base, so guilty, so—[*Sees key in his desk, down R., runs and opens it, and is about to rummage among the papers when* JULIUS *enters at L. and observes her.*]

Julius. Ahem! [*She shuts the desk and stands confused.*] Don't let me disturb you. You are at home, of course.

Una. [R.] I thought—I thought the desk was empty, and I wanted to get an envelope.

Jul. I see—you expected to find an envelope in an empty desk.

Una. I mean, I wanted to put away some articles, and I suddenly remembered that this was not our room. [*Aside, going up.*] I'll look—I'll rummage everywhere. [*Exits, R. U. D.*]

Jul. Jealous! And Fred is heartbroken. These two hearts must be reunited. I have composed a neat little note to set them going. [*Takes an envelope out of his pocket, opens it, draws forth a letter and reads.*] "My sweetest sweet, your letter received. Shall expect you to-morrow at six at the Benedick. Yours for the past, present, and future—BEATRICE. Monday the 8th." [*Speaks as he replaces letter in envelope.*] My innocent bachelor flat in the Benedick shall appear to Una as the siren's bower, and to Fred as the tempter's abode. They shall both go there to surprise each other, and the deuce is in it if they don't become reconciled for life. [URQUHART *re-enters, C. L., with small bag open.*]

Urquhart. [L.] Where is Schlagg? I rung and he doesn't answer. I want him to pack my trunks.

Jul. Where are you going?

Urq. I'm going to travel. I suppose I may travel?

Jul. How far?

Urq. Alaska. [Schlagg *enters,* l. c.]

Schlagg. Did you ring, sir?

Urq. [*Giving him bag.*] Pack my trunks. Put all my warm things in.

Schl. [c.] Yes, sir.

Urq. We start to-night. [*Crosses,* c.]

Schl. [l.] *We* start. You and me, dat is?

Urq. Yes, for Alaska.

Schl. [*Sulkily.*] I don't know dose places. Who starts mit Alaska to-night?

Urq. You and I. Go along and pack up. [*Goes to desk and looks over papers.*]

Schl. Vould it make some differences if ve did not go until to-morrow?

Urq. Are you crazy?

Schl. I vas very sorry—I cannot start dis evening.

Urq. Why not?

Schl. My vife haf just gome back to me already.

Jul. Don't tear him away. *He* hasn't quarrelled with his wife.

Schl. Ach, my vife and I, ve ain't no better as anybody elses —ve quarrel; ve have words; but ve make it ups. So often ve haf rows, so often ve haf make ups. Ach! it is schweet dose evening togedder ven der is a row over.

Urq. [*Crosses,* c., *half angry.*] That will do.

Schl. Yes, sir.

Urq. You won't come with me?

Schl. My vife has only just come to me.

Urq. Consider yourself discharged—[*Snatches bag from him.*] on the spot. [*Exit,* l. *door.*]

Schl. [*Speaks after him, with folded arms.*] Tyrant! Despot! Czar!

Jul. [*To himself.*] I'll stop this journey. [*Stage,* r.]

Schl. [*Coming forward familiarly.*] Oh, thank you, sir.

Jul. What's that?

Schl. You said you'd stop this journey, and I said thank you.

Jul. Oh! [Una *enters followed by* Antoinette. *She is dressed to go out.*]

Una. Antoinette, get my travelling dress ready. John, get me a coupé.

Schl. [l.] I vish respectfully to gif madam notice dat I am been discharged, and dat I take my vife vid me. De vife go wherefer ther husband go.

Una. Mr. Urquhart discharges you? Come to me. I engage you.

Ant. Oh, merci, madame. [*Exit, R. U. D.*]

Jul. [R.] That will make a hole in your four dollars.

Una. [*To* SCHLAGG.] Now call a coupé. [SCHLAGG *starts.*]

Jul. Going for that divorce?

Una. I'm going on a journey. [SCHLAGG *stops.*]

Jul. Where?

Una. [*Crosses, R.*] To Canada.

Jul. With four dollars? People who go to Canada usually start with more than four dollars.

Una. I have borrowed Antoinette's savings. She goes with me.

Schl. I beg pardon, but my vife haf just been restored to me, and if ve start to-night——

Jul. [L.] You're in hard luck, Schlagg. Go and get that coupé.

Schl. Ve see! Canada! My vife she congeal dere. [*Exit, c.*]

Jul. So you are really going away?

Una. [*Sits, R.*] Does it incommode you?

Jul. Not in the least.

Una. I believe I have the right!

Jul. [*Aside.*] Now for the march to the train!

Una. I consider myself quite free to do as I please.

Jul. Certainly. Of course the divorce can wait until you come back, and in that case I needn't give you this—[*Taking note from his pocket.*] until you return.

Una. [*Rises.*] What is it?

Jul. It's of no consequence, unless you were determined on having the divorce at once.

Una. I can stop at the lawyer's on my way to the depot.

Jul. [*Tantalizingly.*] Oh, there's no hurry.

Una. Come, what have you got there? [*Tries to read the letter over his shoulder. He ostentatiously puts it behind him as she goes on his L.*]

Jul. Something Fred thought might be useful in your suit. It's not important till the trial comes off.

Una. Let me see it!

Jul. Fred expects, of course, that your lawyer will find your case insufficient, as you have no proofs, and being as eager as you to get the divorce as quickly as possible, he asked me to give you this, which removes every difficulty.

Una. [*Snatches the letter and crosses*, R.] Give it to me!

Jul. [*Rubbing his hands and chuckling. She turns and almost catches him.*] I think you will agree with me that it leaves no room for doubt. [*Turns and faces her.*]

Una. [*Reads.*] "My sweetest sweet." [*Looks at him.*] "Your letter received. Shall expect you to-morrow at six, at the Benedick—Beatrice. Monday, the 8th." [*Speaks.*] The 8th was yesterday. [*Breathless.*] The appointment is for to-day.

Jul. Yes, to-day at six. That is what we may call something tangible.

Una. [*Much excited.*] This explains how he knew all about the *flagrante delictu.* He had one on hand. It was for this creature he refused to insult my mother.

Jul. The intention was good.

Una. Who is this person—this Beatrice? Do you know her? Who is she?

Jul. [*Aside.*] She can manufacture a story. Let me try.

Una. Tell me all.

Jul. I believe she's from the South—a Mexican. I think Mexico is quite south.

Una. A southern Mexican! Her name! Her real name!

Jul. Anastasia! That's her real name. She's the wife of a major-general in the Mexican army, now visiting in New York—Major-General Palo Alto Cerro Gordo.

Una. [*Crossing*, L., *and back to* C.] Mrs. Major-General Anastasia Palo Alto Cerro Gordo! Oh, the wretch! [*Weeping.*] Where does she live?

Jul. At the Benedick Flats, corner of Sixth Avenue and Sixty-ninth Street. Take the elevator.

Una. The "Benedick!" [*Weeps.*] I shall remember. [*Crosses up*, R.]

Jul. You don't thank me.

Una. [*Very woebegone.*] Thank you. Oh! Oh! Oh! [*Exit*, R. U. D.]

Jul. She'll be there at six o'clock. The next thing is to send Fred there. But he knows my writing.

Schlagg. [C. L., *Enters and announces.*] Dr. Hoffman! [*Exits.* HOFFMAN *enters*, C.]

Jul. Ah, Charley! [*Holds out his hand.*]

Hoffman. [*Holding him back with his hat, then clasping his hands behind him.*] Excuse me, I must content myself with a merely formal recognition.

Jul. [*Imitating his manner.*] I return the salute.

Hoff. Miss Jenny refuses to marry me until her sisters are taken back by their husbands. My happiness is at stake for no fault of my own. I have come to ask you to take back your wife to oblige Jenny and me.

Jul. This introduces a new complication.

Hoff. My patients are suffering.

Jul. And an element of danger for life.

Hoff. [*With a whine and an outburst, falls on* JULIUS' *neck.*] Oh, you don't know how wretched I am.

Jul. Yes, I do. I was engaged once. You'll get over it. [*Struck with an idea, slaps him on the back.*] The very man. Will you do me a favor?

Hoff. [*Still whining.*] No.

Jul. Then sit down here and write as I dictate. I pledge you my solemn vow that if you do, it as good as marries you to Jenny.

Hoff. [*Hopefully.*] Does it? As good as marries me? [*Sits, R., at desk.*]

Jul. It does. [*Puts paper, ink, etc., before him, and hands him a pen.*] I only want you to write a short note.

Hoff. Go on. [*Rhoda is passing from R. door to C., stops in surprise at the words "Darlingest Darling."*]

Jul. [*Dictating.*] "My Darlingest Darling. [HOFFMAN *looks up in surprise;* JULIUS *signs him to proceed. He does so, repeating each half line after* JULIUS.] "You know that I love you, and if glances do not deceive, I feel that I am loved in return."

Rhoda. [*Aside.*] Oh, heavens!

Jul. "As nothing separates us now, will you not grant me one interview—" [HOFFMAN *looks up,* JULIUS *speaks.*] Oh, you'll marry Jenny. This as good as marries her to you already. [*Dictates.*] "I shall expect you at my rooms at six o'clock to-day. Yours—yours, always and ever yours." [*Speaks*]. Put a lot of exclamation marks.

Hoff. [*Writes.*] Exclamation marks.

Jul. Sign, Major-General Palo Alto Cerro Gordo.

Hoff. [*Looks up.*] Why Palo Alto? Your name isn't Palo Alto Cerro Gordo.

Jul. Yes it is. It's my *nom de souper* when I go on a lark. [HOFFMAN *writes.*]

Rho. [*Aside.*] The little wretch! His *nom de souper.*

Jul. Palo Alto Cerro Gordo. Now the date and address, "The Benedick, Sixth Avenue and Sixty-ninth Street."

Rho. The Benedick, Sixth Avenue and Sixty-ninth Street!

Hoff. Ah! This as good as marries me to Jenny!

Jul. [*Seizes the letter, reads it over with a chuckle, blots it, folds it. Aside, going as* RHODA *disappears.*] And now I shall tell Fred that I found this in his wife's room. [*Exit,* L. D.]

Hoff. He doesn't even thank me.

Rho. [*Bursting in furiously and glaring toward door where* JULIUS *went out.*] He has a *flagrante delictu,* too. He goes by a false name. He has private lodgings of his own. Major-General Palo Alto Cerro Gordo! Another outrage upon our Mexican neighbors. Oh!

Hoff. [R., *Rises timidly.*] Mrs. Naggitt——

Rho. [*Advancing scornfully.*] A nice business you are . engaged in. Leave me, sir. [*He tries to speak.*] Not a word. Leave me. [*Crosses,* R.]

Hoff. [*Aside, going.*] Never mind. I'm as good as married to Jenny. [*Exits,* C. L.]

Rho. [*Alone.*] The Benedick! Six o'clock! At six o'clock there'll be three at that rendezvous. [*Exit,* R. SCHLAGG, L., *and* ANTOINETTE, C., *appear at opposite doors.*]

Schlagg. [L.] Pst! Tony! Pst!

Antoinette. Pst! [*They are about to rush into each other's arms.*]

Schl. At last, after two weeks, we are alone.

Ant. Alone! [SCHLAGG *about to kiss her when* JOBLOTS *enters,* C. L.]

Joblots. No one to show me up! [SCHLAGG *and* ANTOINETTE *fly apart.* ANTOINETTE *exits,* R.] Where are my daughters?

Schl. Och! I know noding.

Job. [C., *Sinks in chair.*] I feel remorse. They may be at this moment wandering the streets like the two orphans. [*To* SCHLAGG.] My wife is below in a hansom. She is crying. Even the cabman is affected. I wish to know if my sons-in-law had the cruelty to let my daughters depart. [UNA *enters,* R. D.] Una!

Una. [*Falls on his neck, weeping.*] Oh, papa! oh! oh! [SCHLAGG *exits,* L. D.]

Job. My poor child, calm yourself. Your father is left to you. So is your mother. She is below in a hansom, and she is crying. And the cabman is crying, too.

Una. [*Full of horror.*] Oh, if you knew!

Job. Is there something else?

Una. [*Crosses,* L.] My husband is false. He's got a - grante delictu.

Job. Fred! Impossible!

Una. Mrs. Major-General Palo Alto Cerro Gordo, Sixth Avenue and Sixty-ninth Street, six o'clock. [*Crosses,* R.]

Job. [*Looks at his watch.*] You are dreaming!

Una. I wish I was. But I have proof. [*Takes out letter and crumples it in her hand.*] Proofs, papa. Oh, papa! don't be surprised at anything you hear. I feel I am going mad. [*Crosses,* R.] It's emotional insanity I know. [*Crosses,* L., *up.*] Remember that when I am on trial, I'm going to kill her—kill him—kill 'em both—both—both—kill 'em both! [*Exits,* L. C.]

Job. Kill them! Rash child! What a day! Sixth Avenue and Sixty-ninth Street. Oh, Una! Una! Both! both! Kill 'em both! [*Exit,* L. C. SCHLAGG *and* ANTOINETTE *appear as before and rush into each other's arms.*]

Schlagg. Mein Lieben!

Antoinette. After two weeks! [*About to kiss her, when* URQUHART *is heard outside. Both fly apart and exeunt,* SCHLAGG, L., *and* ANTOINETTE, R., *as* URQUHART *and* MRS. JOBLOTS *enter,* C.]

Urquhart. [*Very angry; walks all round room with the letter written by* HOFFMAN *open in his hand.*] Such a letter to my wife! [*Calls at door,* R.] Una! [*Opens it.*] She is gone! There is no room for doubt! [*Throws himself in chair,* L.]

Mrs. Joblots. [*Greatly agitated, following* URQUHART *from door to door.*] What is going on? First Una came down, then Jeremiah; he shouted, "Go home," and fled up the street like mad. Where have they gone?

Urq. [*Rises.*] Do you wish to know where Una is going? [*Crosses,* R.]

Mrs. J. Yes.

Urq. Read that. [*Gives her letter.*]

Mrs. J. Um—um—Six o'clock—Yours always—Major-General Palo Alto——

Urq. Cerro Gordo! Yes. At the Benedick, Sixth Avenue and Sixty-ninth Street. Your daughter has gone to meet him.

Mrs. J. A daughter of mine! You are taking leave of your senses!

Urq. We shall see. I'm going too. [*Crosses round sofa.*]

Mrs. J. Do.

Urq. There'll be three at that rendezvous.

Mrs. J. Good!

Urq. And I shall kill 'em—all—all—[*Exit,* C.]

Mrs. J. Kill 'em all! [*Screams and falls on sofa in strong hysterics.* HOFFMAN *runs in,* C., SCHLAGG, L., *and* ANTOINETTE, R.]

Schlagg. Run for a doctor!

Hoffman. I'm a doctor!

Mrs. J. [*Seizes both his hands.*] Doctor! [*Gasping.*]
The—the Benedick——

Hoff. Yes——

Mrs. J. Sixth Avenue and Sixty-ninth Street.

Hoff. Yes——

Mrs. J. Six o'clock—I must be there,

Hoff. You can't! You're too weak!

Mrs. J. Carry me! [HOFFMAN *swings her into seat,* L. C.,
which SCHLAGG *puts forward.*]

Hoff. This as good as marries me to Jenny! [*He and*
SCHLAGG *pick up the chair with* MRS. JOBLOTS *and carry her off,*
ANTOINETTE *following and fanning her.*]

QUICK CURTAIN.

ACT III.

SCENE.—*An apartment in the " Benedick Flats ; "* L. C., *an
arch at the back showing an inner room and an opening,
C., looking on a staircase. Table, C., with writing uten-
sils. Chandelier and suspended lamp. Sofa and easy
chairs scattered about. Screen up* R. *Doors,* R. *and* L.
1 E. *and* R. C. *Window,* L. C.

Julius. [*Enters,* C., *rubbing his hands, and in quite good spir-
its, looks round, rings bell on table.*] It's all right. Nothing to
do but let them in when they call ; and I've got the daughter
of the porter to act as my housekeeper for the day, answer the
bell and refuse to answer anything else. She belongs to the
American Conservatory and Metropolitan School of Amateur
Acting, but otherwise she seems to be bright, intelligent, and
capable. Her father's name is Tucks, but we call her Myrtilla.
[MYRTILLA *sings outside.*] There she is now. [*Rings again.*
The American Conservatory has much to answer for. [*Rings*]
again. MYRTILLA *enters, quite brightly dressed.*]

Myrtilla. [L., *Drops a courtesy.*] Did you ring, sir ?

Jul. [*Seated.*] Yes. How does your new part suit you so
far ?

Myr. [L., *Gushingly.*] It's just in my style. Nothing to
do, no one to wait on even, for nobody ever comes.

Jul. You'll have plenty of work to-day. You'll have to open
the door twice.

Myr. Is that all?

Jul. [*Rises.*] No.

Myr. Oh! the work's beginning to be harder than I thought.

Jul. Listen. Two persons will call—separately. One a gentleman, the other a lady.

Myr. [L.] Good enough. [*Nods.*]

Jul. The gentleman may bounce in like a bombshell. [*She starts back.*] Don't be afraid of him. If he begins to break the furniture, simply get out of his way.

Myr. I'm to let him do it.

Jul. Yes. He may behave himself. He may simply ask for Major-General Palo Alto Cerro Gordo. Tell him he's out and ask him to wait. [*Sitting on corner of table.*]

Myr. That's easy.

Jul. He may inquire if a lady has called. If the lady *has* arrived before him, tell him "Yes."

Myr. And if the lady has not arrived I'm to tell him "No."

Jul. You've got it like a book. [*Crosses, L.*]

Myr. It's not hard. In fact, only simple truth.

Jul. The lady may appear excited, and she also may bounce in like a bombshell.

Myr. That makes two bombshells.

Jul. [*Sitting L. of table.*] Or she may act like a well-bred, sensible person, for she happens to be one, and she comes after her husband. She also will ask for Major-General Palo Alto Cerro Gordo.

Myr. Ah, she is Mrs. Major-General Palo Alto Cerro Gordo.

Jul. No. She is not.

Myr. When will Mrs. Major-General What's-her-name come?

Jul. Mrs. Major-General Palo Alto and so forth will never come. There is no such person. I am the Major-General and Mrs. Major-General Palo, etc., etc. When she asks for me, tell her I'm out, and ask her to wait.

Myr. Well, if she don't come.

Jul. [*Not heeding.*] If she inquires whether a gentleman has arrived, you will answer yes or no, according to the fact.

Myr. Then I'm to act toward the lady exactly as I act toward the gentleman?

Jul. Precisely, and when they are both here, you will leave them together. [*Crosses, L.*]

Myr. Shall I ask 'em if they want dinner?

Jul. Certainly. Let them have plenty of ice-water and crackers. If you hear a row pay no attention. They are hus-

4

band and wife, and they have a few conundrums to put to each other. Be attentive, careful, *and* discreet, and you will receive fifty dollars per week, with a chance of promotion. [MYRTILLA *gasps with joy. Aside.*] I only want her a week.

Myr. Oh! Thank you!

Jul. One more important detail. If either or both of them try to hide from the other, let them do it. If necessary, assist. [*Bell heard very violently.*]

Myr. Number one.

Jul. [L.] Open the door. I'll take the back stairs. Above all, discretion—and remember the cues in the part I've given you. Don't stick, for I shan't be here to prompt you.

Myr. Oh, I won't stick. [*Exits singing up* R. *Off* C. L.]

Jul. She is evidently studying for soubrette. [*Bell heard.*] She stops. She's at the door. A man's voice. I vanish. [*Exit lower door.*, L. H.]

Urquhart. [*Bursts into room at* C., *followed by* MYRTILLA.] Major-General Palo Alto Cerro Gordo!

Myr. [*At back.*] I told you he was gone out. [URQUHART *searches about the room.*] Bombshell number one.

Urq. Gone out, is he? Gone out where?

Myr. [*Down*, R.] Don't ask conundrums. You can wait.

Urq. I intend to. Are you alone?

Myr. How alone?

Urq. Is there no one else here?

Myr. Yes.

Urq. [*Grasps her. In a hoarse whisper.*] Who?

Myr. You! [*He throws her off.*]

Urq. I mean who else is in the house besides us?

Myr. There's a family on every floor.

Urq. Stupid! Is there any one else on this flat but you and me?

Myr. Nobody! I swear it! [*Melodramatically.*]

Urq. [*Pulling her round.*] Idiot! [*Facing her.*] And pray how is this master of yours—this Major-General *Palo Alto Cerro Gordo*, as he calls himself?

Myr. [R.] He's pretty well.

Urq. The girl's a fool. Is he young? Is he old? What's he like? Can you pull your senses together and describe him? Let me see his picture!

Myr. I haven't got his picture. He never gave me his photograph. But he's lovely; not at all like you. [URQUHART *crosses*, R.] A regular ladies' man!

Urq. The girl is hopeless! Is there a Mrs. Major-General Palo Alto?

Myr. Oh, yes !

Urq. Where is she ?

Myr. Gone out with him.

Urq. He must be quite an original, to make an appointment n his own house, with his wife likely to pop in at any moment. My wife, of course, will pretend that she came to visit his wife. Ha ! ha ! A blind ! [*To* MYRTILLA.] Listen to me ! [*Pulls her round and faces her brusquely.*]

Myr. I've been listening ; but you mumbled so I could only catch a word here and there.

Urq. [*Giving her money.*] Idiot child ! here are five dollars.

Myr. [L.] They are only worth seventy-seven and three-fourth cents on the dollar. [*Drops them into her pocket.*]

Urq. Listen. [*She puts her hand to her ear to listen. He pulls her hand down.*] Answer me : Doesn't your master expect a lady this afternoon ?

Myr. He does.

Urq. That's all I wish to know. [*Crosses,* L., *round, and starts off in a fury.*]

Myr. Then five dollars are too much. I'll give you back the change.

Urq. [R., *Pressing her hand back into her pocket.*] No— keep it, and conceal me somewhere. When that lady and the major-general are together, come and tell me. [*Crosses,* L.]

Myr. Right away ?

Urq. In five minutes ! No—two minutes. On second thought—come and tell me instantly.

Myr. I'll show you to a room off the entry. It's nothing more than a closet ; but you won't be dull, there's a Webster's Dictionary on the shelf. [*Bell.*] Here comes the lady. [*Goes to apartment at back and points to door,* L.] You go that way. I'll let her in. [*Exit singing.* L. C., *Dancing around front table.*]

Urq. And that girl can sing while a terrible tragedy hovers over these gilded salons. [*Goes up and listens.*] I can't hear the voice, it's too low. Let's be sure it *is* she, and then— [*Goes behind the screen.*]

[JOBLOTS *enters, followed by* MYRTILLA.]

Joblots. [R., *Taking a card from his card-case.*] I wish to see Mrs. Major-General Palo Alto Cerro Gordo, if you please. Here is my card.

Urq. [*Looks over the screen.*] Poor old gentleman ! his wife must have told him.

Myrtilla. [L., *Reads card.*] Mr. Jeremiah Joblots. [*Aside*] This complicates matters. I had no instructions about *him*. [*Aloud.*] She's gone out, sir.

Job. I'll wait for her.

Myr. Very sorry, but I can't allow you to do that.

Job. Is the major-general in?

Myr. No, sir.

Job. Then I'll wait for him.

Myr. Can't allow that neither.

Job. [*Slips a coin in her hand.*] Here's half a dollar for you. Lend me a pen and a sheet of paper. [*Aside.*] I will write a letter to the misguided woman who is luring my son-in-law to destruction. [*Sits at table and helps himself to ink, paper, etc.*]

Myr. He takes it easy. [*Bites the money to test it.*]

Job. [*Writes.*] "Madame : It is a father who addresses you. I implore you to consider my daughter's happiness. Give up my son-in-law and accept the inclosed check for one thousand"—[*Pauses a moment and crosses it.*] No—"five hundred" —[*Same business.*] No—"two hundred and fifty;" yes, "two hundred and fifty dollars. Respectfully." [*Pauses, then crosses it out.*] No—"Cordially"—[*Same business.*] No— "Sincerely"—[*Same business.*] No——

Myr. [*Kneeling on chair by table.*] Better make up your mind to one or the other.

Job. [*Writes.*] "Truly yours, Jeremiah Joblots." [*Puts letter in envelope and directs it.*] "Mrs. Major-General Palo Alto Cerro Gordo." [*Rises and gives it to* MYRTILLA.] Here, my child. [*Chucks her under the chin.*] Sweet innocent! Hand this to your mistress, and when Mr. Urquhart comes——

Myr. [L.] I don't know any Mr. Urquhart.

Job. [R.] I understand all about that. You are paid to know nothing. I haven't sat on the front row of the orchestra all my life not to know how this sort of thing is managed. But I have paid you fifty cents to be honest, and you mustn't try to deceive me. Listen ! [*Crosses,* L.] Be attentive. [*Goes to window.*] I am going to the restaurant on the opposite corner. When Mr. Urquhart—[MYRTILLA *makes a gesture.*] I know you are going to tell me again you don't know him, but nevertheless when he comes place yourself here and wave something —[*Gets to window.*] something conspicuous—a tablecloth, or anything.

Myr. And all that for half a dollar !

Job. [*Giving money.*] Here, take a dollar.

Myr. [*Examines it.*] It's only half a dollar.

Job. And half a dollar before makes a dollar. [*Exits,* c. l.]

Myr. A dollar! I won't wave anything but a handkerchief.

Urquhart. [*Comes from behind screen.*] Here are five dollars more. You'll wave nothing at all. [*Gives her silver money.*]

Myr. [l.] All right. [*Pockets the money.*]

Urq. He gave you a letter. Give it to me.

Myr. But——

Urq. Here's five dollars more. [*Giving money.*]

Myr. If I should fall overboard now, I'd sink. [*Crosses,* r.]

Urq. [*Taking letter from* Myrtilla.] I will return the letter to its proper owner. Have no fear. [*Pockets it as the bell rings violently.*] There's a ring.

Myr. Go to your dictionary. [*Bell rings again, very furiously.*] I'm coming! I'm coming! Off with you! [*Opens door up* r. *for* Urquhart.]

Urq. Don't forget to let me know the moment they are together. [*Bell again violently rung. He exits.*]

Myr. Oh, can't you have patience? [*Exits, singing.*] The bell goes a-ringing for Sarah. [*Bell is heard ringing all the time. It suddenly stops; a door is heard to slam; voices in altercation, and* Myrtilla *comes flying back before the impetuous entrance of* Una, *who dashes around the whole room, examining every corner. Her veil is partly down; it is rather a heavy one.*]

Una. Where are they? The cowards! The vile, miserable creature! Oh, you needn't hide. I'll find you. Not a soul! [*Sinks in chair.*] Not a shadow!

Myr. [*Timidly,* r. *of table.*] Bombshell number two. [*Advancing.*] Do you wish to see anybody, madam?

Una. I wish to see your mistress. [*Starting.*]

Myr. She's out.

Una. I'll wait till she comes in.

Myr. Yes, ma'm.

Una. Describe her!

Myr. Describe her?

Una. How does she look? What is she like?

Myr. [*Crosses,* l., *strutting.*] Oh! awful stylish!

Una. [r.] Oh! [*Hand to heart.*] Here! [*Takes out her pocket-book.*] Take this pocket-book. It contains four dollars and a postage-stamp. And now tell me, is she married?

Myr. Oh, yes, indeed!

Una. Does her husband live with her?

Myr. Of course.

Una. Fred will pretend that he came to see the husband. [*Bell heard.*] Hide me! Hide me quick! [*Runs up,* c.]

Myr. No, no, here! [*Puts her in* R. 1 E. *Feeling the pocket-book.*] If that sort of thing goes on I'll soon be able to invest in real estate. [*Exit,* C. L., *singing a lively air.*]

Una. [*Reappears at door.*] I can't hear a word. It must be he.

Mrs. Joblots. [*Outside.*] I will go up.

Una. No, it is she. [*Disappears.*]

Mrs. J. [*Enters,* C., *followed by* Myrtilla, *is quite hyster-ical.*] My child, my innocent child! Give me back my inno-cent child! [*Facing* Myrtilla.]

Myr. [R.] I haven't got your child. Whom are you look-ing for?

Mrs. J. My child is not guilty. She is only headstrong. [*Sinks in chair,* R. C. Myrtilla *fans her with a magazine.*]

Hoffman. [L., *Entering,* C., *after* Mrs. Joblots.] Where can she be?

Mrs. J. Why did you come up? I told you to stay in the cab. I don't want you to pollute your young mind with this dreadful business. [*Rises.*]

Hoff. [*Crosses to her.*] But I know everything already, and I beg you to come away. This is no place for you.

Mrs. J. A mother's place is beside her child when that child is in danger.

Myr. [L., *Aside.*] He didn't tell me anything about all these people. What am I to do with 'em? [*Aloud, to* Mrs. Joblots.] Haven't you made some mistake, ma'am? Whom do you wish to see?

Mrs. J. [*Crosses,* C.] I wish to see your master, the major-general.

Hoff. You're right. It is better to see him. Suppose I take charge of the matter on your behalf?

Mrs. J. But first—my daughter. Has she got here yet?

Hoff. [R., *Surprised.*] Was she to come?

Mrs. J. Yes; nothing could prevent her. Stop. [*Goes to table and writes.*]

Hoff. [*Up stage,* R. *Beckons to* Myrtilla.] Is the lady here?

Myr. Yes. In there. [*Points to* R. 1 E., *and gets back,* L.]

Hoff. Thanks. [*Goes to door,* R. 1 E., *and bolts it.*] There!

Mrs. J. [*Reads.*] "Sir, it is a mother who addresses you. Spare a wretched parent her daughter who was married but eighteen months in October, and believe me yours, ever grate-fully." [*Folds it and puts it in an envelope. To* Myrtilla, *who looks on with open-mouthed wonder as she is licking the gum side.*] You don't know the feelings of a grown-up mother with her wretched daughters. [*Writes address.*] Major-General Palo Alto Cerro Gordo. [*Hands it to* MYRTILLA.] Give this to your master as soon as possible, and when the lady comes—[*With emotion, wringing her handkerchief.*] tell her that her mother is waiting for her in the basement. [*Exits,* c. l.]

Hoff. [*To* MYRTILLA, *sternly.*] Now then, where is Mr. Naggitt?

Myr. Mister who?

Hoff. Mr. Naggitt. Come, come, don't play innocent. I know everything.

Myr. Do you? That's where you have the advantage. If you'll explain——

Hoff. Listen. Mr. Naggitt, your master, is fooling his wife. He told me so himself.

Myr. But I don't know any Mr. Naggitt. I'm engaged here by Major-General Palo Alto——

Hoff. Cerro Gordo! I know. You are employed by a Mr. Julius Naggitt, who calls himself Cerro Gordo when he goes on a lark. But there's no necessity to make a noise. Simply tell your master when he comes that his wife and his mother-in-law know everything.

Myr. [*Crestfallen.*] Proceed.

Hoff. And tell them that I am waiting in the basement.

Myr. I can't promise anything. My head's buzzing. [*Crosses,* R.]

Rhoda. [*Enters,* c. *As soon as she sees the others she lowers a heavy veil over her face.*] He here too?

Hoff. [*To* MYRTILLA.] I thought you told me the lady was in there?

Myr. [*On seeing* RHODA *throws up both hands.*] What, another? That's enough! No more for me! I'm through! [*Darts out,* c. l.]

Hoff. [*As* RHODA *goes down,* L.] Madam! I have not the honor of your acquaintance, but I am the friend of your friend, Mr. Naggitt; in fact, I'm almost his brother-in-law. I wish to warn you that his wife knows all.

Rho. [L., *Raises her veil.*] Thank you.

Hoff. Mrs. Naggitt!

Rho. I see you continue to lend your assistance to my husband in this vile business. Leave the house.

Hoff. But please—only listen to one word.

Rho. Silence.

Hoff. Julius told me it as good as married me to Jenny.

Rho. Indeed! Well, take my word for it, you may say good-by to Jenny and all hopes in that quarter. [*Stage,* L.]

Hoff.   Can Julius have deceived me?

Rho.   He deceives everybody, his wife included.

Hoff.   Then he'll get caught now, and serve him right. Good-morning!   [*Exit,* c.]

Una.   [*Shakes door,* R.] Open the door! I hear you in there!

Rho.   A woman's voice!

Una.   Open, I say!

Rho.   It must be his darlingest darling.   [*Lowers her veil, while* UNA *rattles at the door.*]   Enter, madam! [*Opens the door,* UNA *bursts in, and both speak at the same time.*]

Una.   Where's——

Una and Rho.   My husband!

Rho.   [*Raising her veil.*] Una!

Una.   Rhoda!

Rho.   What are you doing here?

Una.   What are *you* doing here?

Rho.   Julius is false, I have the proof.

Una.   Fred is deceiving me. I have the proofs. [*Crosses,* L.] She is to meet him here at six o'clock.

Rho.   So is Julius.

Una.   [*Closing on her.*] This is why they wanted a divorce. I'm going to faint! Air! Give me air! [*Goes to window, throws it open, and fans herself with handkerchief.*] The wretches! to want to get rid of us so soon.

Rho.   They want a divorce, do they! *We'll* get a divorce and marry someone else.

Una.   No, I won't. I've had quite enough. [*Breaking down.*] And I loved him so!

Rho.   [*Also breaking down.*] So did I!

Una.   And in two weeks he forgets me for Mrs. Major-General Anastasia Palo Alto Cerro Gordo. [*Bell.*]

Rho.   Here they come. [*They pull down their veils and stand on each side the* c. *door.*] The wretches!

Joblots.   [*Enters,* c., *followed by* MYRTILLA.] Now, then, where is he?

Myrtilla.   Where is who?

Job.   You gave me the signal at the window.

Myr.   I? [*Goes and closes window.*]

Una and Rho.   [*As they unveil.*] Papa!

Job.   Una! Rhoda! [*They throw themselves in his arms.*]

Una.   Both our husbands have deceived us. [MYRTILLA *exits with uplifted hands.*]

Job.   Both?

Una.   [*Rousing herself.*] Papa, call a policeman! [*Crosses,* L.]

Job. Be calm!

Rho. [*Also rousing herself.*] Call two policemen—[*Crosses,* R.] and have both of 'em taken up!

Job. I will call your mother, who is weeping in the basement.

Rho. Why don't the wretches come? Perhaps they have been warned. [*Bell heard. They run up, crossing at back.*]

Una. At last! [*Lowers her veil;* RHODA *does the same. They stand aside,* R. *and* L., *of* C. *door, as* JULIUS *enters.*]

Julius. [*Enters cautiously.*] Pst! Myrtilla! Pst! Pst! Myrtilla! Where are you?

Rho. [*Aside.*] My little wretch, I'll give him Myrtilla! [*Approaches from behind and gives him a box on the ear just as he turns up stage.*]

Jul. Oh! Who the deuce are you?

Rho. [R., *Unveils.*] Who am I?

Jul. [L.] My wife!

Rho. Your wife! who begs the honor of an introduction to your Myrtilla, or whatever she calls herself, on the instant.

Jul. My dear, you are mistaken.

Rho. Mistaken, you imp! [*About to seize his ear,* JULIUS *retreats down stage, and gets,* R. *She restrains herself.*] I won't touch you, don't be afraid; you'd make a point of it in court. But I'll find your Myrtilla, no matter where you hide her. [*Exits,* C., UNA *throws herself in chair,* R, *sobbing.*]

Jul. Who is that? Una, of course. Good. [*Goes to her.*] My dear young lady. [*She lifts her veil, he affects to be surprised.*] Dear me! why, Mrs. Urquhart! Have you seen your husband yet?

Una. [*Decisively.*] Not yet, the monster! But I'm waiting for him.

Jul. [*Aside.*] What can Myrtilla be doing? Fred must be here somewhere. [MYRTILLA *enters,* C., *peering round the room, and seeing* JULIUS, *flies to him.*]

Myrtilla. Ah! One familiar face at last! [*Seizes both hands, shakes them effusively, and smuggles to his side.*]

Jul. [*Getting,* C., *to avoid her.*] Don't do that. [*Moves off.*] Where's the gentleman?

Myr. The gentleman? Which one? Oh! [*Recollecting.*] In the dictionary closet. [*Points off* R. U. *door.*]

Jul. Go and call him.

Myr. He told me to come and tell him when you and the lady were together. But I am so mixed. There's been a regular circus here since you went away. Such a lot of people! Old people, young people, tall, short, lean, fat, masculine, feminine—all sorts. I am bewildered. [*Stage,* L.]

Jul.   What are you raving about?   [*Crosses,* R.]

Una.   [*Seated,* L., *to* MYRTILLA.]   Will you please go and tell Mr. Urquhart?

Myr.   I don't know Mr. Urquhart.

Jul.   It's the gentleman in the closet.   **Go.**

Myr.   Oh! I see!   [*Staring at* UNA.]

Jul.   Go at once!

Myr.   Right off.   [*Darts off,* R. U. *door.*]

Una.   [*Reproachfully.*]   You, too, are deceiving your wife.

Jul.   [*Solemnly.*]   I swear——

Una.   Don't swear!   She has proofs!

Jul.   Has she?   Then I'm off!   [URQUHART *heard outside.*] There's Fred!   [*Darts off* L. 1 E. *and locks it as* URQUHART *enters* L. U. E., *and seeing the figure disappear dashes after it.*]

Urquhart.   You scoundrel!   [*Shaking the door and trying to force it.*]   I'll find you yet!

Una.   [*As he turns and faces her, she advances.*]   Now, sir! I suppose you'll tell me you came to see the general, and not his wife!

Urq.   I certainly did.

Una.   I was sure of it.

Urq.   And you came to see the wife and not the general?

Una.   Certainly!   The brazen hussey!

Urq.   Enough of this.   Your presence and mine in this place explains all.

Una.   [*Stage,* R.]   I should think so.   [MR. *and* MRS. JOB-LOTS *speak outside in hot dispute.*]

Joblots.   [*Outside.*]   Let us find them.

Mrs. Joblots.   No use of shouting.   [*Enters,* C.]

Joblots.   [*Entering.*]   Let us have a full understanding.

Mrs. J.   It's my right to question my daughter first.   [*Advancing to* UNA, *sternly.*]   Una!   What are you doing here?

Una.   [R.]   I have been waiting for him!   [*Points to* URQU-HART.]

Mrs. J.   [R. C.]   Unhappy child!   You know you were waiting for Major-General Palo Alto Cerro Gordo.

Una.   [*Quickly.*]   No—his wife.

Urq.   [*Laughs.*]   As I foresaw.   Luckily, I read this letter.

Job.   [L. C.]   She is right.   She is waiting for the wife—the woman who has lured Frederick on to destruction.

Urq.   I beg pardon!   Lured me?

Mrs. J.   No, darling.   I read his letter to her.

Una.   [*To* MRS. JOBLOTS.]   What letter?

Job.   Yes, what letter?

Mrs. J. A letter from the general, which Frederick gave me to read.

Urq. Exactly.

Job. [*To* Urquhart.] Do you know this Mexican?

Urq. The fellow just escaped me. He was warned by *her* in time.

Mrs. J. My child, beg your husband's pardon and promise never to do so any more.

Una. Pardon! For what?

Urq. [*Crosses,* c.] For what? [*Indignantly.*] What are you doing here?

Una. Watching you!

Job. Yes—you!

Una. And your Anastasia—your sweetest sweet Mexican.

Urq. My Anastasia? *My Mexican?*

Una. [*To others.*] Why, he sent me her letter himself by his brother-in-law.

Urq. [*Angrily.*] What letter?

Una. Her letter to you making an appointment for six o'clock to-day.

Rhoda. [*Re-enters,* c.] I can't find anybody.

Mrs. J. Rhoda! Where did you come from?

Rho. [c.] I came to catch them.

Mrs. J. Came to catch your sister?

Rho. [*Crosses to* Mrs. Joblots.] My sister? How you talk, mamma. No, Julius—Julius and his Myrtilla.

Mrs. J. [*Looks at* Joblots, *and both look at the others, then back at* Rhoda.] What are you talking about?

Rho. [*Breaking into tears.*] It's nothing but the truth.

Job. [*Placing all the others at intervals on either side so as to catechise each clearly.*] Stop a bit. Let's get this thing into some kind of shape. [*Back to audience and speaking to* Rhoda.] You say your husband has a Myrtilla?

Una. And she lives here! I saw her!

Mrs. J. [*To* Urquhart.] I shouldn't be surprised if that was your Mexican!

Urq. Madam!

Mrs. J. Keep your temper!

Urq. It was Julius gave me the letter from that military fellow to my wife.

Job. Stop. [*To* Rhoda.] What led you to suspect your husband?

Rho. I heard him dictating a letter to Dr. Hoffman, making a rendezvous at this house for six o'clock to-day.

Mrs. J. Then she lives here—with the general.

Rho. Of course she does.

Job. Then the general is married?

Una. Of course he is.

Mrs. J. And Julius is in love with the general's wife?

Una. No, no; Frederick is in love with her.

Rho. No, no; don't you understand? Julius is the general himself.

All. Ah!

Job. This is enough to drive a man crazy. [*All but* RHODA *go up stage in despair and give up the problem.*]

Hoffman. [*Entering,* c.] Oh, Mr. Joblots, I'm so glad I found you.

Job. He'll explain. [*Seizes* HOFFMAN *by one hand.*]

Rho. My witness. [*Seizes the other.*]

Mrs. J. Your witness!

Rho. He wrote the letter. [*To* HOFFMAN.] Be frank. Yes or no. Does my husband correspond with another person?

Hoff. I—I——

Rho. Speak out!

All. [c.] Speak out!

Hoff. Well, I did write a letter at his dictation, but I wouldn't have done it if he hadn't said it as good as married me to Jenny.

Job. [*Severely.*] Where is that letter?

Hoff. I gave it to Julius, of course, and he sent it.

Urq. Where?

Hoff. I don't know.

Una. [*Crosses to him.*] But you wrote it?

Hoff. I wrote the letter, not the address.

Job. So much for that letter. [*Crosses to* MRS. JOBLOTS.] Now for the letter you saw.

Mrs. J. That's it.

Job. [*Crosses to* URQUHART.] And the one you saw!

Urq. That's it.

Job. [*Crosses to* RHODA.] And Rhoda's letter?

Hoff. That's it. Same one.

Job. [c.] I thought I'd untangle it. The whole thing's as plain as a pipe-stem. Julius corresponds with an unknown female, and gets the doctor to write his letters.

Rho. [*Impatiently.*] That's what I said.

Una. But how about the letter I saw? The letter from the hussey herself? [JOBLOTS *about to take it,* URQUHART *snatches it, down on* R. *of* UNA.]

Urq. Don't know it. Never saw the woman's handwriting before. [*It is passed round to all rapidly, who speak in turn.*]

Omnes. "I don't know it." "Never saw it." "No." "Wholly unfamiliar," etc.

Una. [*To whom the letter is finally restored.*] Do you deny your guilt? [*To* URQUHART.]

Urq. Certainly I do.

Una. In the face of this? It's too much!

Mrs. J. [*Crosses to* HOFFMAN.] As for you, doctor, I am surprised that you should help Julius in his equivocal correspondence.

Hoff. [*Appealingly to* JOBLOTS.] Upon my word and honor, as I stand here, I did it all for the best. Julius said it as good as married me to Jenny.

Job. You are a serpent, sir, whom I will never take by the hand as a son-in-law. [*Waves him off.*]

Hoff. I'm ruined! Oh Jenny! Jenny! [*Rushes out,* R., *and nearly collides with* MYRTILLA, *who enters and announces.*]

Myrtilla. Mr. and Mrs. Major-General Palo Alto Cerro Gordo.

Omnes. At last! Now we'll see! [*All turn their backs to front as* JULIUS *enters,* O., *hat in hand.*]

Julius. Ladies and gentlemen, good afternoon!

All. Julius!

Jul. Yes, Julius, who played this little game in order to prove to this gentleman—[*Indicating* URQUHART.] that he was desperately in love with his wife, and to this lady—[*Pointing to* UNA, C.] that she was hopelessly infatuated with her husband. Their mutual jealousy proves the fact. The letter which I dictated to our young friend, the doctor, I myself handed to Fred.

Urq. [L.] That's true.

Jul. And I gave the letter which I wrote myself in a disguised hand to you. [*To* UNA.] Now kiss and make up. [*Seeing them hesitate.*] Well?

Urq. [*To* UNA.] Can you——

Una. Forgive me? [*Seizes her in his arms.*]

Urq. How I have made you suffer! The fault was wholly mine.

Una. Hush! Let the blame be mine. [*As they are going up stage lovingly, she looks back over her shoulder to her sister.*] Rhoda!

Rho. Well?

Una. Do as I do; they are too much for us.

Rho. [*To* JULIUS, *who has been eyeing her quizzically.*] Well, aren't you going to say anything?

Jul. [*Taking her round her waist.*] How I've made you suffer!

Rho. The fault was mine.

Jul. No it wasn't—it was mine.

Rho. No, mine.

Jul. Well, we'll toss up for blame. [*They go aside,* R.]

Jenny. [*Outside.*] Are you sure?

Hoffman. [*Outside.*] Sure.

Mrs. J. Jenny's voice!

Job. I believe it is. [JENNY *enters with* HOFFMAN *and* MYR-TILLA.]

Myr. [*Announcing.*] Two more bombshells.

Jenny. [*Flies to her father and mother and kisses them.*] Oh, mamma! Oh, papa! I'm so glad to find you again. I thought you'd never come home. I was so frightened, and I took Sarah and went to sister Rhoda's husband's house and found that he had moved, then I went to sister Una's husband's house and found that you had all come up here, and we came up here, too, and just as we got near here, whom should we run across but Charley—Doctor Charles, I mean—in an awful state of desperation, but I persuaded him to return with me and all would be explained.

Job. It has been! It has been! Charley, you may marry my only remaining daughter.

Hoff. [*Crosses to* JENNY, *both get,* R.] Shall I? Then I am as good as married already.

Mrs. J. Your sisters and their husbands are reconciled.

Jenny. Are you sure? For good?

Mrs. J. We shall see.

Urq. [*Advancing with* UNA.] I have the honor to ask for the hand of your daughter.

Rho. [*To* JULIUS.] If Frederick does, I'm sure *you* ought to.

Jul. [*To* URQUHART.] That's both rhyme and reason, eh, old chappie? Behold us, too! [*Advances with* RHODA.]

Una. Behold us four! [*All kneel.*]

Urq. And make us happy!

Rho. We promise faithfully to never more distress you.

Job. On that condition, children, bless you! bless you! [*All rise.*]

Mrs. J. Oh, how it comforts me to see this cooing.
The Manual did it, and it's all my doing.
Here! [*Thrusts book into* UNA's *hand.*]
You find it. See page twenty;
There are fitting sentiments in plenty.

Una. [*Turns to page.*] "Divorce proceedings."

Mrs. J. [*Annoyed.*] No, turn over.

Una. [*Turns page.*] "How to keep a husband still a lover."

Mrs. J. Ah!

Job. Don't speak unkindly.

Jul. At least don't bawl.

Urq. Don't contradict.

Jul. In fact, don't talk at all.

Hoff. Hush!

Una. "Let every wife recall what first enchanted,
What grace, what look, what temper love inspired.
You were his ideal once, and, take for granted,
You will be still, if still what he admired."

Urq. My notion, too.

Jul. It's all the women's fault.

Urq. We're not to blame.

Jul. Not the least bit.

Hoff. Halt!

Una. [*Reads.*] "For the men"—
"To go in 'double harness' is your pet
Phrase for wedlock. Pray, don't forget
That means side by side, or better yet,
A tandem! One may lead, but both must strive,
And neither, mark me! *neither* one must drive."